USA TODAY bestselling author **Barb Han** lives in north Texas with her very own hero-worthy husband, three beautiful children, a spunky golden retriever/standard poodle mix and too many books in her to-read pile. In her downtime, she plays video games and spends much of her time on or around a basketball court. She loves interacting with readers and is grateful for their support. You can reach her at barbhan.com.

Discover more at millsandboon.co.uk.

Texas Law
BARB HAN

MILLS & BOON

First published in Great Britain 2020
by Mills & Boon, an imprint of HarperCollins*Publishers*
1 London Bridge Street, London, SE1 9GF

Large Print edition 2020

© 2020 Barb Han

ISBN: 978-0-263-29331-9

MIX
Paper from
responsible sources
FSC
www.fsc.org **FSC C007454**

This book is produced from independently certified FSC™ paper to ensure responsible forest management. For more information visit www.harpercollins.co.uk/green.

Printed and bound in Great Britain
by CPI Group (UK) Ltd, Croydon, CR0 4YY

All my love to Brandon, Jacob and Tori, the three great loves of my life.

To Babe, my hero, for being my best friend, my greatest love and my place to call home.

I love you all with everything that I am.

Chapter One

Sheriff Colton O'Connor took a sip of coffee and gripped the steering wheel of his SUV. Thunder boomed and rain came down in sheets. Seeing much past the front bumper was basically impossible. He'd had three stranded vehicle calls already—one of those cars had been actually submerged—and the worst of this spring thunderstorm hadn't happened yet. The storm wreaking havoc on the small town of Katy Gulch, Texas, was just getting started.

On top of everything, Colton's babysitter had quit last night. Miss Marla's niece had been in a car crash in Austin and needed her aunt to care for her during her recovery. The spry sixty-five-year-old was the only living relative of the girl, who was a student at the University of Texas at Austin.

Colton pinched the bridge of his nose to stem the thundering headache working up behind his eyelids. His mother was pinch-hitting with his twin boys, Silas and Sebastian, but she was still reeling from the loss of her husband, as was Colton and the rest of the family.

A recent kidnapping attempt had dredged up the unsolved, decades-old mystery of his sister's abduction, and his father was murdered after deciding to take it upon himself to take up the investigation on his own again. Colton was just getting started untangling his father's murder.

Considering all that was going on at the ranch, Colton didn't want to add to his mother's stress. As much as his one-year-olds were angels, taking care of little ones with more energy than brain development was a lot for anyone to handle. His mother had enough on her plate already, but she'd convinced him the distraction would be good for her.

And now a storm threatened to turn the town upside down with tornadoes and flash floods.

So, no, Colton didn't feel right about leaving his mother to care for his children, although Margaret O'Connor was strong, one of the toughest women he'd ever met.

He took another sip of coffee and nearly spit it out. It was cold. Bitter. The convenience-store kind that he was certain had been made hours ago and left to burn. That tacky, unpleasant taste stuck to the roof of his mouth.

This might be a good time to stop by the ranch to check on his mother and the twins. He could get a decent cup of coffee there and he wanted to check on his boys. His stomach growled. A reminder that he'd been working emergencies most of the night and had skipped dinner. He always brought food with him on nights like these, but he could save it for later. It was getting late.

Colton banked a U-turn at the corner of Misty Creek and Apple Blossom Drive, and then headed toward the ranch. He hadn't made it a block when he got the next call. The distinct voice belonging to his secretary, Gert Francis, came through the radio.

"What do you have for me?" He pulled his vehicle onto the side of the road. At least there were no cars on the streets. He hoped folks listened to the emergency alerts and stayed put.

"A call just came in from Mrs. Dillon. Flood waters are rising near the river. She's evacuating. Her concern is about a vagrant who has been sleeping in her old RV. She doesn't want the person to be caught unaware if the water keeps rising, and she's scared to disturb whoever it is on her own." Mrs. Dillon, widowed last year at the age of seventy-eight, had a son in Little Rock who'd been trying to convince her to move closer to him. She had refused. Katy Gulch was home.

Colton always made a point of stopping by her place on his way home to check on one of his favorite residents. It was the happiest part of his job, the fact that he kept all the residents in his town and county safe. He took great pride in his work and had a special place in his heart for the senior residents in his community.

He was a rancher by birth and a sheriff by choice. Both jobs had ingrained in him a commitment to help others, along with a healthy respect for Mother Nature.

Colton heaved a sigh. Thinking about ranching brought him back to his family's situation. With his father, the patriarch of Katy Bull Ranch, now gone, Colton and his brothers had some hard decisions to make about keeping their legacy running.

"Let Mrs. Dillon know I'm on my way." Actually, there was no reason he couldn't call her himself. "Never mind, Gert. I've got her number right here. I've been meaning to ask her how she's been getting around after foot surgery last week."

"Will do, Sheriff." There was so much pride in her voice. She'd always been vocal about how much she appreciated the fact he looked after the town's residents. The last sheriff hadn't been so diligent. Gert had made her opinion known about him, as well.

"After I make this call, I need to check

out for a little while to stop by the ranch and see about things there," he informed her.

"Sounds like a plan, sir." More of that admiration came through the line.

Colton hoped he could live up to it.

"Be safe out there," Gert warned.

"You know I will. I better ring her now." Colton ended the call. Using Bluetooth technology, he called Mrs. Dillon. She picked up on the first ring.

"I hear you have a new tenant in the RV. I'm on my way over." Colton didn't need to identify himself. He was pretty certain Mrs. Dillon had his cell number on speed dial. He didn't mind. If a quick call to him or Gert could give her peace of mind, inconvenience was a small price to pay.

"Thank you for checking it out for me. This one showed up three nights ago, I think." Concern came through in Mrs. Dillon's voice. "I know it's a woman because MaryBeth's dog kept barking and I heard her tell him to shush."

"Well, if she stays any longer you'll have to start charging rent," he teased, trying to lighten the mood.

The older woman's heart was as big as the great state they lived in.

"If I started doing that, I'd end up a rich lady. Then all the young bachelors would come to town to court me. We can't have that, can we?" Her smile came through in her voice.

"No, ma'am. We sure can't."

"I hope she's okay." She said on a sigh. "Not a peep from her. I wouldn't have heard her at all if it hadn't been for MaryBeth's dog." Mrs. Dillon clucked her tongue in disapproval. Normally, her neighbor's dog was a thorn in her side. This time, Cooper seemed to have served a purpose.

"Sounds like we have a quiet one on our hands. I'll perform a wellness check and make sure she gets out before the water rises."

"I always complained to my husband that he put the parking pad to the RV way too close to the water's edge. But do you think he listened?" Her tone was half-teasing, half-wistful. Mr. and Mrs. Dillon had been high school sweethearts and had, much like Colton's parents, beaten the odds of divorce and gone the distance. The Dillons had been school-teachers who'd spent their summers touring the country in their RV. Anyone who knew them could see how much they loved each other. They were almost obnoxiously adorable, much like his own parents had been.

Losing Mr. Dillon had to have been the hardest thing she'd gone through. Colton's heart went out to her.

"I just didn't want her to be caught off guard. If this storm is as bad as they say it's going to be, the RV will be flooded again." She heaved a concerned-sounding sigh. "I probably should've gotten rid of that thing ten years ago after the first time it flooded. But Mr. Dillon loved his camping so he could throw out a line first thing with his morning coffee." Her voice was nothing but melancholy now at the memory.

"He was one of the best fishermen in the county." Colton swerved to miss a puddle on the road that was forming a small lake. Flash flooding was a real problem in the spring. This storm was just beginning to dish out its wrath. Mother Nature had a temper and it was becoming apparent she was gearing up to show them just how angry she could become.

"That he was," she agreed.

"Who is driving you to Little Rock?" He changed the subject, hoping to redirect her from a conversation that would bring back the pain of losing her husband. After seeing the look on his mother's face at hearing the news her husband was dead, Colton didn't want to cause that kind of hurt for anyone, certainly not for someone as kind as Mrs. Dillon. His second grade teacher deserved more brightness in her day, and especially after putting up with him and his brothers when they were young. They'd been good kids by most standards. And yet they'd also been a handful. After having twins, Colton was more aware of the responsibility and sacrifice that came with the parenting job.

"Netty. You know her from my knitting club. She's heading that way to stay with her daughter, so I'm hitching a ride with her." He could almost see the twinkle in Mrs. Dillon's eye when she said the word *hitched.*

"Tell Netty to drive safe." He could barely see in the driving rain and needed to close the call in order to concentrate on the road ahead.

"I will do it, Sheriff. Thank you for checking on my *tenant*." He could envision her making air quotes when she said the last word.

"You're welcome. In fact, I'll head to your house now." After exchanging goodbyes, he ended the call.

The rain was so thick he could barely see the end of his vehicle now, let alone the road. The weather had definitely turned in the last couple of minutes since he'd started the conversation.

It was a miracle he could see at all. His headlights were almost useless. If he didn't know the area so well, he'd pull over and wait it out. These kinds of storms usually came in waves. Radar didn't look promising on this one.

As he turned right onto Mrs. Dillon's street, a flash of lightning streaked across the sky, and a dark object cut in front of him so suddenly he couldn't stop himself from tapping it with his service vehicle.

A *thunk* sounded and then a squeal. The noise was quickly drowned out by the driving rain.

Colton cursed his luck, wondering if he'd been struck by debris. He hopped out of his vehicle to check. Rain pelted his face. He pulled up his collar and shivered against the cold front, praying whatever he'd hit wasn't an animal. Deer sometimes cut through town. At least he was on his way to the ranch. He could scoop it up, put it in the back and see what he could do about nursing it back to health.

Pulling his flashlight from his belt, he shined it around the area. It was next to impossible to see. Hell, he could barely see his hand in front of his face for the rain.

Squinting, he caught sight of something moving a few feet from his passenger-side bumper. Hell's bells. He hadn't nicked an animal at all…it was a person.

Colton dashed to the victim. He took a knee beside the woman, who was curled in a tight ball. Her dark clothing covered her from nearly head to toe. She was drenched and lying in a puddle.

"My name is Colton O'Connor. I'm the sheriff and I'm here to help." He knew better than to touch her in case she was injured.

"I'm okay. You can go." He didn't recognize the voice, but then it was next to impossible to hear over the sounds of the rain. She kept her face turned in the opposite direction, away from him.

Considering she seemed anxious to not show her face to him, he wondered if she had something to hide.

"I'm not going anywhere until I know you're okay. And that means being able to stand up and walk away from here on your own," he said, figuring she might as well know where he stood.

"I already said that I'm okay. Go away," the woman shouted, and he heard her loud and clear this time. Her voice was somewhat familiar and yet he couldn't place it.

He dashed toward his vehicle and retrieved an umbrella. It wouldn't do much good against the torrent. Water was building up on the sidewalk and gushing over faster than the gutter could handle it. But it was something and might help with some of the onslaught.

And he believed that right up until he opened the umbrella and it nearly shot out of his hands. A gust of wind forced him to fight to hold on to it and keep it steady over the victim. Finally, it was doing a good job offering some shelter from the rain.

"Like I said, I need to see that you can walk away from here on your own and answer a few questions. I'm the one who hit you and there's no way I'm leaving. What's your name?" He bent down lower so she could hear without him shouting at her.

She didn't answer and that sent up more warning flares. Anyone could see she was injured. She'd taken a pretty hard hit. She might be in shock or maybe suffering head trauma. From his position, it was impossible to see if she was bleeding, and because of the way she'd fallen, he couldn't rule out a broken arm or leg.

Colton stood up and walked around to where she was facing. He dropped down on his knees to get a better look. Rain was everywhere—his eyes, his ears, his face. He shook his head, trying to shake off the flood.

"I'm calling an ambulance. I'm going to get some help." He strained to see her face, still unable to reach back to his memory and find a name that matched the voice. In a small town like Katy Gulch, Colton knew most everyone, which meant she was someone who'd passed through town.

She lifted her arm to wave him away.

"No can do. Sorry." He tilted his mouth toward the radio clipped to his shoulder. With his free hand, he pressed the talk button. "Gert, can you read me?"

There was a moment of crackling. He feared he might not be able to hear her response. And yet going to his SUV wasn't an option. He didn't want to leave the woman alone in the street in the soaking rain again. She looked like she needed a hand-up and he had no plans to leave her.

With the wind, his umbrella was doing very little, but it was something.

The woman, who had been curled up on her side, shielding her face, pushed up to sit. "See, I'm okay. I'm not hurt.

I just need a minute to catch my breath and I'll be fine."

Colton wasn't convinced she was able to think clearly. Often after experiencing trauma, it took a while for the brain to catch up. That was how shock worked. She might not even realize it.

"What's your name?" he asked again, trying to assess her mental state.

She shook her head, which either meant she didn't want to disclose it or she couldn't remember. Neither was a good sign.

Since she hadn't answered his question, there was no choice but to have her cleared medically before he could let her go, even if she could walk away on her own, which he highly doubted at the moment.

"I'm just going to get somebody here to take a look at you, and if everything's okay, you'll be cleared in no time. In the meantime, you can wait inside my vehicle and get out of this weather." He'd noticed that she'd started shivering.

He slipped out of his rain jacket and placed it over her shoulders.

The woman looked up at him and their gazes locked. His heart stirred and his breath caught.

"Makena?"

WATER WAS EVERYWHERE, flooding Makena Eden's eyes and ears. Rain hit her face, stinging like fire-ant bites. She blinked up and stared into the eyes of the last man she'd expected to see again—Colton O'Connor.

Still reeling from taking a wrong turn into the road and being clipped by his sport utility, she felt around on her hip.

Ouch. That hurt. She could already feel her side bruising. Mentally, she tried to dust herself off and stand up. Her hip, however, had other plans, so she sat there, trying to ride out the pain.

"I just need a minute." There was no other option but to get up and fake being well. She had no job, no medical insurance and no money. And she couldn't afford to let her identity get out, especially not on a peace officer's radio. Then there was the other shock, the fact that Colton was kneeling down in front of her. How long had it been?

"Not so fast." Colton's eyebrow shot up and he seemed unconvinced. He was one of the most devastatingly handsome men she'd ever met, and her body picked that moment to react to him *and* remind her. This was turning out to be one red-letter day stacked on the back end of months of agony. One she'd survived by hiding and sliding under the radar.

"I don't want you to try to move. We need to get you checked out first." He snapped into action, tilting his chin toward his left shoulder to speak into his radio. She could hear him requesting an ambulance. For a split second, she wondered if she could run away and get far enough out of sight for him to forget this whole situation. *Wishful thinking.* It was so not good that he knew her personally. Granted, he knew her before she'd become Mrs. River Myers, but still...

Panic squeezed her lungs as she tried to breathe through the building anxiety. She couldn't let her name go down on record. She couldn't have anything that would identify her over the radio.

"I promise that I'm not broken. I'm shaken up." Before she could say anything else, he put a hand up to stop her.

Water was dripping everywhere, and yet looking into those cobalt blue eyes sent her flashing back to her sophomore year of college. The two of them had been randomly hooked up as partners in biology lab. Even at nineteen years old, it was easy to see Colton was going to be strong and muscled when he finally filled out.

Now, just seeing him released a dozen butterflies in her chest along with a free-falling sensation she hadn't felt since college. She could stare into his eyes for days. He had a face of hard angles and planes. Full lips covered perfectly straight, white teeth.

Looking at him was like staring at one of those billboard models. The man was tall. Six feet four inches of solid steel and ripped muscle. The only reason she noticed was the survival need at its most basic, she told herself. She was in trouble and had to assess whether or not Colton could defend her.

Icy fingers gripped her spine as she thought about the past, about *her* past. About *River.* Stand still long enough and it would catch up to her. He *would* find her.

Colton might look good. Better than

good, but she wouldn't let her mind go there for long. There were two things that would keep her from the attraction she felt, other than the obvious fact they'd had one class and a flirtation that hadn't gone anywhere. A badge and a gun.

Chapter Two

Makena needed to convince Colton that she wasn't injured so she could get far away from him and Katy Gulch. Coming here had turned out to be a huge mistake—one that could get her killed.

How had she not remembered this was his hometown?

Being on the road for months on end had a way of mixing up weeks. Towns were starting to run together, too. They fell into one of two categories, big and small.

Dallas, Houston and Austin fit into the big-city category. They all had basically the same chain restaurants if a slightly differing view on life. Small towns, on the other hand, seemed to share a few characteristics. In those, she was beginning to realize, it was a little harder to go unnoticed.

Getting seen was bad for her longevity.

The other thing she'd noticed about small towns in her home state of Texas was the food. Some of the best cooking came from diners and mom-and-pop shops. Since she'd run out of money, she'd been forced to live on other people's generosity.

Makena hadn't eaten a real meal in the past three days. She'd sustained herself on scraps. The owner of the RV where she'd been staying had been kind enough to leave a few supplies and leftovers a couple of days ago, and Makena had stretched them out to make them last. Hunger had caught up to her, forcing her to seek out food.

The fact that the owner knew Makena

was staying on her property *and* Makena had remained there anyway signaled just how much she'd been slipping lately. Starvation had a way of breeding desperation. Not to mention it had been so very long since she'd slept on a real bed in a real room or in a real house that she could scarcely remember how it felt. The RV was the closest she'd come and she hadn't wanted to give it up.

Makena was drenched. She shivered despite having the sheriff's windbreaker wrapped around her. She could sit there and be stubborn and cold. Or, she could get Colton's help inside the SUV and wring herself out. And at least maybe have him turn the heat on.

"If you help me up, I can make it to your vehicle," she said to him.

Colton's eyebrow shot up. "You sure it's a good idea to move? I didn't realize how badly you were hurt when I offered before."

"I'm so cold my teeth are chattering. You look pretty miserable. There's no reason for me to sit here in a puddle when I can be warm inside your vehicle." She had to practically shout to be heard. She put her hands up in the surrender position, palms up. "All I need is a hand up and maybe a little help walking."

He opened his mouth to protest.

"Sitting out here, I may end up with the death of cold." She realized she was going to have to give him a little bit more than that. "I'm pretty sure that I have a nasty bruise working up on my left hip. It was stupid of me to run into the street. I didn't even see you."

"You must've darted out from in between the parked vehicles right when I turned." There was so much torment in his voice now.

"Sorry. I was just trying to stay out of the rain but I'm okay. Really." It wasn't a total lie. Mostly, a half-truth. Being dishonest pained Makena. She hated that she'd become the kind of person who had to cover her tracks like a criminal.

"What are you doing out on a night like this?" he asked.

"I-um…was trying to get back to my rental over by the river." The way she stammered was giving her away based on the look on his face.

He nodded as he studied her, but she could see that he wasn't convinced.

"My name is Makena. You already know that. It's Wednesday. At least, I think it is."

"Do you know where you are right now?" The worry lines on his forehead were easing up.

"Katy Gulch, Texas," she said. "And I've been out of work for a little while. That's the reason I've lost track of the days of the week."

It was her turn to look carefully at him.

"What do you think?" she asked. "Did I pass?"

Colton surveyed her for a long moment. Lightning raced sideways across the sky and thunder boomed.

"Lean on me and let me do the heavy lifting." He put his arm out.

"Deal." She grabbed hold of his arm, ignoring the electrical impulses vibrating up her arm from contact. This wasn't the time for an inappropriate attraction and especially not with a man who had a gun and a badge on his hip. She'd been there. Done that. And had the emotional scars to prove it.

Not taking Colton's help was out of the question. She had no car. No money. No choices.

Makena held onto his arm for dear life. As soon as she was pulled up to her feet, her left leg gave out under the pain from her hip.

"Whoa there." Colton's strong arms

wrapped around her, and the next thing she knew he'd picked her up. He carried her over to his SUV and managed to open the passenger door and help her inside.

She eased onto the seat and immediately felt around for the adjuster lever. Her fingers landed on the control and she adjusted her seat back, easing some of the pressure from her sitting bones. Her hip rewarded her by lightening up on some of the pain.

Colton opened the back hatch, closed it and was in the driver's seat a few seconds later.

He then leaned over and tucked a warm blanket around her. "Is that better?"

"Much." She said the word on a sigh, releasing the breath she'd been holding.

"Be honest. How badly does it hurt?" he asked, looking at her with those cobalt blues.

"On a scale of one to ten? I'd say this has to be a solid sixteen."

The engine was still humming and at least she'd stopped shivering. She could also finally hear him over the roar of the weather, even though it seemed the rain was driving down even harder than a few minutes ago.

"I couldn't hear a word Gert said earlier." He flashed his eyes at her. "Gert is my secretary in case you hadn't sorted it out for yourself. And she's a lot more than that. She's more like my right arm. I'm the sheriff."

She glanced down at the word *SHERIFF* written in bold yellow letters running down her left sleeve. Even if he hadn't told her earlier, she would've figured it out. With a small smile, she said, "I put that together for myself."

"Is your car around here somewhere? I can call a tow."

"No." Talking about herself wasn't

good. The less information she gave, the better. She hoped he would just drop the subject, let her warm up and then let her get back to her temporary shelter in the RV.

Her stomach growled, and surprisingly, it could be heard over the thunder boom outside.

"There's someone I need to check on. Are you hungry?" Colton asked.

"Yes. I didn't get a chance to eat dinner yet." She followed his gaze to the clock on the dashboard. It read 8:30 p.m.

With his left hand, he tucked his chin to his left shoulder and hit some type of button. "Gert, can you read me?"

Crackling noises came through the radio. And then a voice.

"Copy that, Sheriff. Loud and clear." The woman sounded older, mid-sixties if Makena had to guess.

"I need an ambulance on the corner of Misty Creek and Apple Blossom. Stat. A pedestrian was struck by my vehicle and needs immediate medical attention. She is alert and communicative, with a possible injury to her left hip. She's lucid, but a concussion can't be ruled out," he said.

"Roger that, Sheriff. You must not have heard me earlier. There's flooding on several roads. Both of my EMTs are on calls and even if they weren't, the streets aren't clear. No one can get to you for at least the next hour."

Relief washed over Makena. However, Colton didn't look thrilled.

"Roger that." He blew out a frustrated-sounding breath. "I'll drive the victim to the hospital myself."

"County road isn't clear. There's been a lot of flooding. I don't advise making that trip unless it's life-threatening," Gert said.

Flash floods in Texas were nothing to take lightly. They were the leading cause of weather-related deaths in the state.

"We probably need to close the road since the water's rising," she continued.

Colton smacked his flat palm against the steering wheel. "Roger that."

"As soon as I warm up, you can drop me off. I think my hip just needs a little chance to rest." Embarrassingly enough, her stomach picked that moment to gurgle and growl again.

Colton's gaze dropped to her stomach as he reached under the center console of his SUV and pulled something around. A lunchbox?

He unzipped the black box and produced what looked like a sandwich. He opened the Ziploc bag and held it out toward her. "I knew I'd be working late tonight with the storms. So I made extra. You're welcome to this one."

When she didn't immediately reach for the offering, he locked gazes with her. "Go ahead. Take it. I have more."

"I really can't take all your food." Her mouth was practically watering.

"It's no big deal. I can always swing by my house and get more. It's on the way to my office, not far from here."

"Are you sure about that, Colton?" The last thing she wanted to do was take his food and leave him with nothing. The sandwich looked good, though. And she was pretty certain she'd started drooling.

"It's fine," he reassured her with that silky masculine voice that trailed all over her, warming her better than any blanket could.

He urged her to take it, so she did.

"Thank you." She wasted no time demolishing the sandwich. Ham. Delicious.

He barely looked away from the screen on the laptop mounted inside his vehicle as he handed her an apple next.

This time, she didn't argue. Instead, she polished off the fruit in a matter of seconds while he studied the map on the screen. Just as she wrapped the remains of the apple in the paper towel he'd given her, he pulled out a thermos and handed her a spoon.

"Soup," was all he said.

Angel was all she thought.

COLTON ENTERED the hospital's location into his computer. The screen showed red triangles with exclamation points in the center of them on more roads than not, indicating flooding or hazardous road conditions. Gert was a lifeline, going well above and beyond typical secretary duties. She'd become Colton's right arm and he had no idea what he'd do without her.

Makena needed medical attention. That part was obvious. The tricky part was going to be getting her looked at. He was still trying to wrap his mind around the fact Makena Eden was sitting in his SUV.

Talk about a blast from the past and a missed opportunity. But he couldn't think about that right now when she was injured. At least she was eating. That had to be a good sign.

When she'd tried to stand, she'd gone down pretty fast and hard. She'd winced in pain and he'd scooped her up and brought her to his vehicle. He knew better than to move an injured person. In this case, however, there was no choice.

The victim was alert and cognizant of what was going on. A quick visual scan of her body revealed nothing obviously broken. No bones were sticking out. She complained about her hip and he figured there could be something there. At the very least, she needed an X-ray.

Since getting to the county hospital looked impossible at least in the short run and his apartment was close by, he decided taking her there might be for the best until the roads cleared. He could get her out of his uncomfortable vehicle and onto a soft couch.

Normally, he wouldn't take a stranger to his home, but this was Makena. And even though he hadn't seen her in forever, she'd been special to him at one time.

He still needed to check on the RV for Mrs. Dillon…and then it dawned on him. Was Makena the 'tenant' the widow had been talking about earlier?

"Are you staying in town?" he asked, hoping to get her to volunteer the information. It was possible that she'd fallen on hard times and needed a place to hang her head for a couple of nights.

"I've been staying in a friend's RV," she said. So, she was the 'tenant' Mrs. Dillon mentioned.

It was good seeing Makena again. At five feet five inches, she had a body made for sinning, underneath a thick head of black hair. He remembered how shiny and wavy her hair used to be. Even soaked with water, it didn't look much different now.

She had the most honest set of pale blue eyes—eyes the color of the sky on an early summer morning. She had the kind of eyes that he could stare into all day. It had been like that before, too.

But that was a long time ago. And despite the lightning bolt that had struck him square in the chest when she turned to face him, this relationship was purely professional.

Colton wasn't in the market to replace his wife, Rebecca, anytime soon. He was still reeling from the loss almost year later. He bit back a remark on the irony of running into someone he'd had a crush on in college but not enough confidence to ask out. He'd been with Makena for all of fifteen or twenty minutes now and the surge of attraction he'd felt before had returned with full force, much like the out-of-control thunderstorm bearing down on them.

He refocused. His medical experience amounted to knowing how to perform CPR and that was about it.

Even soaked to the bone, Makena was still stunning—just as stunning as he remembered from twelve years ago in biology lab.

However, it was troublesome just how quickly she'd munched down on the sandwich and apple that he'd given her. She'd practically mewled with pleasure when she'd taken the first sip of soup, which she'd destroyed just as quickly.

Colton glanced at the third finger on her left hand. There was no ring and no tan line. For reasons he couldn't explain, given the fact he hadn't seen Makena in years, relief washed over him and more of that inconvenient attraction surged.

No ring, no husband.

It didn't exactly mean she was single. He told himself the reason he wanted to know was for the investigation. Here she'd shown up in town out of nowhere. She was staying in an RV and, based on the brightness in her eyes, he was certain she was sober. He hadn't expected her to be doing drugs or drinking. However, his job had trained him to look for those reasons first when dealing with uncharacteristic behavior.

Darting across the road without looking, in the middle of one of the worst thunderstorms so far this year, definitely qualified as uncharacteristic. Now that he'd determined she fell into that camp without a simple explanation, it was time to investigate what she was really doing in town and why.

Again, the questions he was about to ask were all for the sake of the investigation, he told himself, despite a little voice in the back of his head calling him out on the lie.

For now, he was able to quiet that annoyance.

Chapter Three

In the dome light, Colton could see that Makena's face was sheet-white and her lips were purple. Color was slowly beginning to return to her creamy cheeks. He took that as a good sign she was starting to warm up and was in overall good health.

"I thought you were in school to study business so you could come back and work on your family's ranch." She turned the tables.

"I realized midway through my degree that my heart was not in business. I switched to criminal justice and never looked back." Colton figured it couldn't hurt to give a little information about himself considering she looked frightened of him and everything else. As much as he didn't like the idea, she might be on the run to something or *from* something. Either way, he planned to get to the bottom of it and give her a hand up. "How about you? Did you stay an education major?"

"I stayed in my field," she said.

He would've thought that he'd just asked for her social security number and her bank passwords for the reaction he got. She crossed her ankles and then her arms. She hugged her elbows tightly against her chest. To say she'd just closed up was a lot like saying dogs liked table scraps over dry food.

"Did I say something wrong?" Colton may as well put it out on the table. He didn't like the idea of stepping on a land mine, and the response he'd gotten from her was like a sucker punch that he didn't want to take twice.

"No. You d-didn't say anything wrong. You j-just caught me off guard." The way she stammered over every other word told him that she wasn't being completely honest. It also made him feel like she was afraid of him, which was strange. Innocent people might get nervous around law enforcement, but straight-up scared? He wasn't used to that with victims.

"Okay. We better get on the road and out of this weather. I promised one of our elderly residents that I would stop by and check on her property. The rain isn't letting up and we're not going too far from here. Her home is nearby. Mind if we—"

"It's okay. You can just let me out. I don't want to get in the way of you doing your job." Panic caused her voice to shake. Colton didn't want to read too much into her reaction.

"Makena, I hit you with my SUV and

the fact is going to bother me to no end until I make absolute certain that you're okay. Check that. I want you to be better than okay. In fact, I'd like to help you out if I can, no matter what you need." He meant those words.

Makena blew out a slow breath. "I'm sorry. You've been nothing but kind. I wasn't trying to put you off. Honest. I'm just shaken up and a little thrown off balance." She turned to look at him, and those clear blue eyes pierced right through him. "Don't take any of this the wrong way. It's just been..." she seemed to be searching for the right words "...a really long time since I've had anyone help me."

Well, he sure as hell hoped she didn't plan on stopping there. If anything, he wanted to know more about her. He chalked it up to nostalgia and the feelings he'd experienced when he was nineteen, the minute he sat beside her in the bio lab, too chicken to pluck up the courage to ask her out.

He'd waited for weeks to see if she felt the same attraction. She was shy back then and he was even shyer. When he finally found his courage, a kid had beaten him to the punch. Dane Kilroy had moved in.

Colton couldn't say he'd ever had the best timing when it came to him and the opposite sex. Missed opportunity had him wanting to help her now. Or maybe it was that lost look in her eyes that appealed to a place deep inside him.

He knew what it was to be broken. His family had experienced a horrific tragedy before he was born. One that had left an echo so strong it could still be heard to this day.

A decades-old kidnapping had impacted the O'Connor family so deeply that they could never be the same again.

The hole could never be filled after his six-month-old sister was abducted.

Colton figured the best place to start with Makena was the basics. "Is your last name still Eden?"

He opened up a file report on his laptop.

"What are you doing?" She seemed shocked.

"Filing a report." Colton forgot that she was a civilian. She would have no idea about the process of filling out an incident report. "I need to file an accident report."

"No. That's really not necessary. I mean, I didn't get a good look at your car but there didn't seem to be any damage to your bumper. As far as me? I'll be okay in a couple of days. There's really no need to file any type of report. Won't that get you in trouble with your job?"

She was worried about him?

"My job isn't going to be on the line

over a freak accident. This is what I do. This is my job, my responsibility."

"What can I say to stop you from filing that report?"

Colton couldn't quite put his finger on what he heard in her tone when she asked the question, but it was enough to send a warning shot through his system.

"Are you in some type of trouble?" he asked.

Part of him wished he could reel those words back in when he heard her gasp. Too late. They were already out there. And consequences be damned, he wanted to know the answer. Maybe he shouldn't have asked the question so directly.

"Colton, this is a bad idea. My hip is hurting right now, but it's going to be fine. There's really no reason to make a huge ordeal out of this. Despite what you said it can't be all that good for your career for you to have a car crash on your record. I can't imagine someone who drives around as part of his job wouldn't be hurt by a report being filed. I promise you, I would tell you if this was a big deal. It's so not."

The old saying, "The lady doth protest too much," came to mind. Colton realized what he heard in her voice. Fear.

And there was no way he was going to walk away from that. "Makena, I can't help you if I don't know what's going on. Do you trust me?"

Colton put it out there. As it was, everything about her body language said she'd closed up. There was no way he was getting any information out of her while she sat like that, unwilling to open up. And since the person closest to a woman was the one most likely to hurt her, as angry as that made him, his first thought went to her hiding out from a relationship that had soured.

Domestic disturbances were also among

the most dangerous calls for anyone working law enforcement.

"It's really nothing, Colton. We're making too big a deal out of this. I'm just passing through town." She heaved a sigh and pulled the blanket up to her neck. "You asked if I stayed with teaching as my degree and the answer is yes. I did. Until the music program was cut from the school where I worked, and I decided to see if I could make it as a musician on my own."

"Really?"

"I've been traveling across the state playing gigs as often as I can set them up. I don't have a manager and I've been living in an RV without the owner's permission, but I planned to leave a note and some money as soon as I'm able to." He noticed her fingers working the hem of the blanket. "I've fallen on hard times recently and jobs have been in short supply.

Really, it's only a matter of time before I get back on my feet."

"Sounds like a hard life and one that's causing you to make tough choices. And the owner knows you've been staying there. She asked me to make sure you're okay." Colton nodded his head. Her explanation nearly covered all the ground of any question he could've thought of. She'd pretty much wrapped up her lifestyle in a bow and the reason she would be moving around the state. But was her story tied up a little too neatly?

He decided to play along for just a minute.

"I thought I remembered seeing you on campus a million years ago picking at a guitar." He tried not to be obvious about watching her response.

"You saw me?" The flush to her cheeks was sexy as hell. She was even more beautiful when she was embarrassed. But that physical beauty was only a small part of her draw. She was intelligent and funny and talented, from what he remembered years ago.

He wondered how much of that had changed...how much she'd changed.

Thunder rumbled and it felt like the sky literally opened up and dumped buckets of rain on them.

Tornado alarms blared. He owed his former father-in-law a call. It was impossible to know if there was an actual tornado or if this was another severe thunderstorm drill. Colton had warned Preston Ellison that overusing the alarm would lead people to disregard it, creating a dangerous situation for residents.

Had the mayor listened?

Clearly not. He hadn't listened to his daughter, Rebecca, either. The single father and mayor of Katy Gulch had overprotected his daughter to the point of smothering her. She'd rebelled. No shock there.

Down deep, Rebecca had always been a good person. She and Colton had been best friends since they were kids and married for less than a year when she'd died. Damned if he didn't miss her to the core some days.

But being with Makena again reminded him why he hadn't married Rebecca straight out of high school.

"ARE YOU COMFORTABLE?" Colton's question felt out of the blue to Makena, but she'd noticed that he'd lost himself in thought for a few minutes as he slogged through the flooded street. This must be his way of rejoining the conversation.

The windshield washers were working double time and had yet to be able to keep up with the onslaught.

"I'm better now that I'm inside your vehicle and we're moving toward safety. Why?" Luckily, the height of the SUV kept the undercarriage of the vehicle above water. The engine sat high enough on the chassis not to flood.

Makena strained to see past the hood. The sirens stopped wailing. The sound would've been earsplitting if it hadn't been for the driving rain drowning out nearly every other sound outside of the SUV.

"The storm's predicted to get worse." He wheeled right and water sloshed as his tires cut a path where he made the turn. The sidewalks of the downtown area and the cobblestoned streets had to be completely flooded now.

"Really?" Makena tried to shift position in her seat so that she could get a good look at the screen he motioned toward. Movement only hurt her hip even more. She winced and bit out a curse.

Colton's laptop was angled toward the driver's side and the only thing she could see was the reflection from the screen in his side window.

He seemed to catch on and said, "Sorry. I can't tilt it any closer to you."

"No need to apologize. Believe it or not, I'm not usually so clumsy, and I don't make a habit of running out in front of vehicles. Like I already said, give this hip a few days and she'll be good as new." Makena forced a smile.

"I hope you weren't planning on going anywhere tonight." There was an ominous quality to his voice, and he didn't pick up on her attempt to lighten the mood.

"Why is that?" Actually, she had hoped to figure out her next move and get back on the road. She'd ducked into the RV to ditch a few friends of her ex-husband, who was the real reason she'd been on the run. Her marriage to an abusive Dallas cop had ended badly. Hunger had caused her to leave the relative safety of the RV. She assumed it would be safer to travel in the rain and easier to cover herself up so she could travel incognito.

It was most likely paranoia, but she could've sworn she'd seen the pair of guys she'd caught in their garage late one night, huddled up and whispering with River. She'd surprised the trio and River had absolutely lost his cool. He'd demanded she go back inside the house and to bed, where he told her to wait for him.

River's decline had become even more apparent after that night. He was almost constantly angry with her over something. Yelling at her instead of talking. Not that he'd been great at it before. Gone was the charm of the early days in their relationship.

When River's attention was turned on, everyone noticed him in the room and he could make the most enigmatic person come to life. River's shadow was a different story altogether. It was a cold, dark cave. His temper had become more and more aggressive to the point she'd had to get out.

"According to radar, this storm's about to get a whole helluva lot worse." Colton's voice cut through her heavy thoughts.

Leaving her husband, River, one year ago had been the best decision she'd ever made. Not a night went by that she didn't fear that he'd find her.

"How is that even possible?" she asked as a tree branch flew in front of the windshield.

"Apparently, Mother Nature isn't done with us yet. We're about to see just about how big this temper tantrum is going to get."

And just when she thought things couldn't get any worse than they already were this evening, the tornado alarms blared again. Rain pounded the front windshield, the roof. And in another moment of pure shock, she realized the winds had shifted. Gusts slammed into the vehicle, rocking it from side to side.

"Normally, I wouldn't leave the scene of an accident. However, if we want to live to see the light of day, we better get out of here." Colton placed the gearshift into Drive and turned his vehicle around. Water sloshed everywhere.

"Where to? You mentioned an elderly neighbor that you need to check on." Another gust of wind blasted the front windshield. Makena gasped.

"She asked me to check on her 'guest' who was staying in her RV. Since you're right here, a change of plans is in order. My place isn't far from here. The parking structure is sound and partially underground. We should be safe there."

Before she could respond, Colton had his secretary on the radio again, updating her on his new destination. Makena figured she could ride out the storm with Colton, giving away as little personal information as she could. Their shared history might work in her favor. Any other law enforcement officer in this situation would most certainly haul her in. Her name would get out.

Makena couldn't risk River figuring out where she was. With his jealous tendencies, it wouldn't be good for him to see her around Colton, either. The Dallas cop would pick up on her attraction faster than a bee could sting.

Colton stopped at the red light on an otherwise empty street. Everyone seemed to have enough sense to stay off the roads tonight. The only reason she'd left the RV at all was to find scraps of food while everyone hunkered down.

Makena had thrown away her phone months ago, so she'd had no idea a storm was on its way. The cloudy sky and humidity had been a dead giveaway but spring thunderstorms in Texas were notorious for popping up seemingly out of nowhere. In general, they retreated just as fast.

This one, however, was just getting started.

Chapter Four

"What do you think?" Colton asked a second time. He'd blame the rain for Makena not hearing him, but she'd been lost to him for a moment.

The prospect of her disappearing on him wasn't especially pleasing. After being in the vehicle with her for half an hour already, he barely knew any more about her or her situation than he had at the start of the conversation.

The fact that she deflected most of his questions and then overexplained told him the storm brewing outside wasn't the only one.

Since she seemed ready to jump if

someone said boo, he figured some things were better left alone. Besides, they were trapped together in a storm that didn't seem to have any intention of letting up over the next twenty-four hours. That would give him enough time to dig around in her story.

Colton relaxed his shoulders. He needed to check in with his mother and see if she was okay with having the twins sleep over. Again, he really didn't like doing that to her under the circumstances no matter how many times she reassured him the twins were nothing but pure joy.

"About what?" Makena asked.

"Staying at my apartment at least until this storm blows over." Colton banked right to avoid a tree limb that was flying through the air.

"When exactly might that be?"

Colton shouldn't laugh but he did. "I'm going to try not to be offended at the fact that you seemed pretty upset about the prospect of spending a couple of hours alone with me. I promise that I'm a decent person."

"No. Don't get me wrong. You've been a godsend and I appreciate the food. I was a drowned rat out there." She blew out another breath. "I wasn't aware there was a big storm coming today. And especially not one of this magnitude. I got caught off guard without an umbrella."

He didn't feel the need to add, without a decent coat. The roads were making it increasingly unsafe to drive to Mrs. Dillon's place. It looked like there were more funnel systems on the way. A tornado watch had just been issued for this and four surrounding counties. He'd like to say the weather was a shock but it seemed folks were glued to the news more and more often every year and some supercell ended up on the radar.

"You didn't answer my question." The

reminder came as she stared at the door handle.

Makena sat still, shifting her gaze to the windshield, where she stared for a long moment. She heaved another sigh and her shoulders seemed to deflate. "I appreciate your hospitality, Colton. I really do. And since it doesn't seem safe to travel in this weather, going to your place seems like the best option. I have one question, though."

"And that is?"

"It's really more of a request." She glanced at the half-full coffee sitting in the cupholder.

He knew exactly what she wanted. "I have plenty of coffee in my apartment. I basically live off the stuff."

"I haven't had a good cup of coffee in longer than I care to count."

His eyebrow must've shot up, because she seemed to feel the need to qualify her statement. "I mean like a really good cup

of coffee. Not like that stuff." She motioned toward the cupholder and wrin-
kled her nose.

He laughed. At least some of the tension between them was breaking up.
There was no relief on the chemistry
pinging between them, though. But he'd
take lighter tension because he was actually pretty worried about her. He couldn't
imagine why she would be living even
temporarily in an RV that didn't belong
to her in a town she didn't know. She
was from Dallas and they'd met in Austin. Again, his thoughts drifted toward
her running away from something—he
wasn't buying the broke musician excuse. And since he hadn't seen her in
well over a decade, he couldn't be one
hundred percent certain she hadn't done
something wrong, no matter how much
his heart protested.

Something about the fear in her eyes
told him that she was on the run from

someone. Who that would be was anyone's guess. She wasn't giving up any information. Keeping tight-lipped might have been the thing that kept her alive. Didn't she say that she'd been on the road for months with her music? There were more holes in that story than in a dozen doughnuts. The very obvious ones had to do with the fact that she had no instrument and no band. He figured it was probably customary to bring at least one of those things on tour.

"To my place then," he said.

The light changed to green. He proceeded through the intersection, doing his level best to keep the questions at bay.

His apartment would normally be a five-minute drive. Battling this weather system, he took a solid fifteen and that was without anyone else on the road. A call home was in order and he needed to prepare Makena for the fact he had children.

As he pulled into the garage and the rain stopped battering his windshield, he parked in his assigned parking spot, number 4, and shut off the engine.

"Before we go inside, I need to make you aware of something—"

Makena scooted up to sit straighter and winced. His gaze dropped to her hip and he figured he had no business letting it linger there.

"Now, there's no reason to panic." It was clear she'd already done just that.

"Was this a bad idea? Do you have a girlfriend or wife in there waiting? I know what you already said but—"

"Before you get too twisted up, hear me out. I have twin sons. They're with my mother because the woman who usually lives with me and takes care of them while I work got called away on a family emergency and had to quit. She hated doing it but was torn, and blood is thicker than water. Besides, I told her to go. She'd regret it if she wasn't there for her niece after the young woman was in a car crash."

"I'm sorry." Much to his surprise, Makena reached over and touched his hand. Electricity pinged. Turned out that the old crush was still alive and well.

"Don't be. It was the right thing for her to do." He debated these next words because he never spoke about his wife to anyone. "I was married. I didn't lie to you before about that. My wife died not long after the babies were born."

"Oh no. I really am sorry, Colton. I had no idea." She looked at him. The pain in her eyes and the compassion in her voice sent a ripple of warmth through him.

He had to look away or risk taking a hit to his heart.

"Why would you?" He'd gotten real good about stuffing his grief down in a place so deep that even he couldn't find it anymore.

When he glanced over at Makena, he saw a tear escape. She ducked her head, chin to chest, and turned her face away from him.

"I'm not trying to upset you…" This was harder than he wanted it to be. "I just didn't want you to walk into my place and be shocked. You've been through enough tonight—" longer if he was right about her situation "—and I didn't want to catch you off guard."

She sat perfectly still, perfectly quiet for a few more long moments. "You have twin boys?"

"Yes, I do. Silas and Sebastian. They are great boys."

When she seemed able to look at him without giving away her emotions, she turned to face him, wincing with movement and then covering. "I bet they're amazing kids, Colton."

It was his turn to smile. "They are."

"Are they at your house?"

"My mom is watching them for me at the family's ranch while I work. She'll be worried with all the weather. I need to check in with her and make sure the boys are asleep."

"How old did you say your boys were?" She seemed to be processing the fact that he was a father.

"One year old. They're great kids." He needed to contact his mother. But first, he needed to get Makena inside his apartment with the least amount of trauma to the hip she'd been favoring. "How about we head inside now?"

He half expected her to change her mind, especially with how squirrelly she'd been so far.

"It would be nice to dry off."

Colton shut off the vehicle's engine and came around to the passenger side. He opened the door. She had her seat belt off despite keeping the blanket around her.

Color was returning to her creamy skin, which was an encouraging sign.

"It might be easier if I just carry you up."

"I think I got it. I definitely need some help walking but I want to try to put some weight on this hip."

Considering Makena knew her identity and didn't slur her speech—a couple of key signs she was lucid—his suspicion that she might have a concussion passed. Although, he'd keep an eye on her to be safe. He figured it wouldn't hurt to let her try to walk; he had to trust her judgment to be able to do that.

"Okay, I'm right here." He put his arm out and she grabbed onto it. More of that electricity, along with warmth, fired through him. Again, he chalked it up to nostalgia. The past. Simpler times.

Makena eased out of the passenger seat, leaning into him to walk. He positioned himself on her left side to make it easier for her. With some effort, she took the first couple of steps, stopping long enough for him to close the car door.

His parking spot was three spaces from the elevator bank, so at least she didn't have far to go.

"You're doing great," he encouraged. He couldn't ignore the awareness that this was the first time in a very long time that he'd felt this strong a draw toward someone. He hadn't been out on a date since losing Rebecca. He'd been too busy missing his wife and taking care of their boys. Twelve months since the kiddos had been born and soon after that, he'd lost his best friend and wife in one fell swoop. He never knew how much twelve months could change his life.

MAKENA LEANED HEAVILY on Colton. She couldn't help but wonder if he felt that same electrical impulse between them. If he did, he was a master at concealment.

Thankfully, the elevator bank was only a few more steps. Pain shot through her if she put any weight on her left leg. But she managed with Colton's help. Despite having told him repeatedly that she'd be fine, this was the first time she felt like it might be true.

The elevator did nothing to prepare her for the largeness of Colton's penthouse apartment. Stepping into the apartment, she realized it took up the entire top floor of the building, which was three stories on top of the parking level.

It felt like she'd been transported into a world of soft, contemporary luxury. "This place is beautiful, Colton."

She pictured him sharing the place with his wife and children. Losing the woman he loved must have been a crushing blow for a man like him. Colton was the kind of person who, once he loved you, would love you forever.

Why did that hurt so much to think about?

Was it because she'd never experienced that kind of unconditional love?

It was impossible not to compare Colton to River. She'd been so young when she and River had gotten together. Too naive to realize he was all charm and no substance. He'd swept her off her feet and asked her to marry him. She'd wanted to believe the fairy tale. She would never make that mistake again.

Colton's apartment comprised one great room and was built in the loft style, complete with a brick wall and lots of windows. The rain thrashed around outside, but the inside felt like a safe haven. In the space cordoned off as the living room, two massive brown leather sofas faced each other in front of a fireplace. In between the sofas was a very soft-looking ottoman in the place of a coffee table. It was tufted, cream-colored and stood on wooden pegs. She noticed all the furniture had soft edges. The light wood flooring was covered by cream rugs, as well.

There was a pair of toy walkers that were perfect for little kids to explore various spots in the room. A large kitchen, separated from the living room by a huge granite island, was to her right. Instead of a formal table, there were chairs tucked around the white granite island, along with a pair of highchairs.

Seeing the kid paraphernalia made it hit home that Colton was a dad. Wow. She took a moment to let that sink in. He gave new meaning to the words *hot dad bod*.

The worry creases in his forehead made more sense now that she knew that he'd lost his wife and was navigating single parenthood alone.

Makena had once believed that she would be a mother by now. A pang of regret stabbed at the thought. She'd known better than to start a family with River once she saw the other side of him. She was by no means too old to start a family except that the pain was still too raw from dealing with a divorce. The dream she'd once had of a husband and kids was the furthest thing from her thoughts as she literally ran for her life. She still felt the bitter betrayal of discovering that the person she'd trusted had turned out to be a monster.

It had taken her years to extract herself from him. Now she'd be damned if she let that man break her. Her definition of happiness had changed sometime in the last few years. She couldn't pinpoint the exact moment her opinion had shifted. Rather than a husband and kids, all she now wanted was a small plot of land, a cozy home and maybe a couple of dogs.

"Are you okay?" His voice brought her back to the present.

"Yes. Your home is beautiful, Colton," she said again.

Now it was his turn to be embarrassed. His cheeks flamed and it was sexy on him.

"I can't take the credit for the decorating. That was my mother." Not his wife? Why did hearing those words send more of those butterflies flittering around in her chest again?

"She did an amazing job. The colors are incredible." There were large-scale art pieces hanging on the walls in the most beautiful teal colors, cream and beige. The woman had decorating skills. The best part was how the place matched Colton's personality to a T. Strong, solid and calm. He was the calm in the storm. It was just his nature.

She took a few more steps inside with his help.

"Can I ask a personal question?" she asked.

He nodded.

"Didn't your wife want to decorate?"

"She's never been here." She felt a wall go up when it came to that subject.

"How about we get you settled on the couch and I get working on that cup of coffee?" he asked, changing the subject. His tone said, case closed.

"Are you kidding me right now? That sounds like heaven." She gripped his arm a little tighter and felt nothing but solid muscle.

He helped her to the couch before moving over to the fireplace wall and flipping a switch that turned it on. There were blue crystals that the fire danced on top of. It was mesmerizing.

She tried to keep her jaw from dropping on the carpet at the sheer beauty of the place. It was selfish, but she liked the fact that he'd only lived here as a bachelor, which was weird because it wasn't like she and Colton had ever dated, despite the signals he'd sent back in the bio lab. She had probably even misread that situation, because he'd never asked her out. The semester had ended and that was that.

Makena again wanted to express to Colton how sorry she was for the loss of his wife. Considering he had one-year-old twins, his wife couldn't have died all that long ago. The emotional scars were probably still very raw.

"If you want to get out of those wet clothes, I can probably find something dry for you to wear for the time being." He seemed to realize how that might sound, because he put his hands up in the air. "I just mean that I have a spare bathrobe of mine you can wear while I throw your clothes through the wash."

She couldn't help herself. She smiled at him. And chuckled just a little bit. "I didn't take it the wrong way and that would be fantastic. Dry clothes and coffee? I'm pretty certain at this point you've reached angel status in my book."

He caught her stare for just a moment. "I can assure you I will never be accused of being an angel."

A thrill of awareness skittered across her skin. A nervous laugh escaped because she hoped that she wasn't giving away her body's reaction to him. "I wouldn't accuse you of that, but I do remember what a good person you are. I wouldn't be here alone with you right now otherwise."

She surprised herself with the comment as he fired off a wink. He motioned toward an adjacent room before disappearing there. He returned a few moments later with a big white plush bathrobe that had some fancy hotel's name embroidered on the left-hand side.

Colton held out the robe. When she took it, their fingers grazed. Big mistake. More of that inconvenient attraction surged. She felt her cheeks flush as warmth traveled through her.

He cleared his throat and said, "I'll go make that coffee now. You can change in here. I promise not to look."

Again, those words shouldn't cause her chest to deflate. She should be grateful, and she was, on some level, that she could trust him not to look when she changed. Was it wrong that she wanted him to at least consider it?

Now she really was being punchy.

Makena took in a deep breath and then slowly exhaled. Colton made a show of turning his back to her and walking toward the kitchen. Despite pain shooting through her with every movement, she slipped out of her clothes and into the bathrobe while seated on the couch. The wreck could've been a whole lot worse, she thought as she managed to slip out of her soaked clothing and then ball it all up along with her undergarments, careful to keep the last part tucked in the center of the wad of clothing.

"Do you still take your coffee with a little bit of sugar and cream?"

"Yes. How did you remember after all this time?"

He mumbled something about having a good memory. Was it wrong to hope that it was a bit more than that? That maybe she'd been somewhat special to Colton? Special enough for him to remember the little things about her, like the fact she took her coffee with cream and sugar?

Logic said yes, but her heart went the opposite route.

Chapter Five

"I'm surprised you don't live on the ranch." Makena watched as Colton crossed the room. He walked with athletic grace. If it was at all possible, he was even hotter than he'd been in college. He'd cornered the market on that whole granite jawline, strong nose and piercing cobalt blue eyes look. Based on the ripples on his chest and arms, he was no stranger to working hard or hitting the gym. His jeans fit snug on lean hips.

"I have a place there where I spend time with the boys on my days off." He handed over a fresh cup of warm coffee.

She took it with both hands and immediately took a sip.

"Mmm. This is quite possibly the best cup of coffee I've ever had."

Colton laughed and took a seat on the opposite couch. He toed off his boots and shook his head, which sent water flying everywhere. He raked his free hand through his hair. He was good-looking in that casual, effortless way. "I got this apartment so I could be closer to my office, after…"

The way his voice trailed off made her think he was going to tell her more about his wife. He shook his head again and recovered with a smile that was a little too forced. He took a sip of coffee. "You don't want to hear my sad story."

Before she could respond, he checked his phone.

"I do, actually," she said softly, but he didn't seem to hear. Strangely, she wanted to hear all about what had happened to him since college. Even then, he'd been too serious for a nineteen-year-old. He'd seemed like he carried the weight of the world on his shoulders. His eyes had always been a little too intense, but when they'd been focused on her they'd caused her body to hum with need—a need she'd been too inexperienced to understand at the time.

He picked up the remote and clicked a button, causing one of the paintings to turn into a massive TV screen. Makena had known his family was successful, but she had no idea they had the kind of money that made TVs appear out of artworks on the wall.

Color her impressed.

It was a shock for many reasons, not the least of which was the fact that Colton was one of the most down-to-earth people she'd ever met. She was vaguely aware of the O'Connor name, having grown up in Texas herself. But being a big-city girl, she had never really been part of the ranching community and had no idea until she'd seen an article about his family years ago. That had been her first hint that they might be wealthier than she'd realized.

Makena had had the opposite kind of childhood. She'd been brought up by a single mother who'd made plenty of sacrifices so that Makena could go to college without having to go into massive debt. And then a couple of years into Makena's marriage with River, long after the shine had worn off and she realized there was no other choice but to get out, her beloved mother had become sick.

Leaving her husband was no longer the number one priority. Her mother had taken precedence over everything else, despite River's protests that helping her ill mother took up too much of her time. He'd had similar complaints about her work, but her job had kept her sanity in check while she watched the woman she loved, the woman whose sacrifices were great, dwindle into nothingness.

Makena reached up and ran her finger along the rose gold flower necklace she wore—a final gift from her mother.

Despite River's protests, Makena remained firm. But with a sick mother who needed almost round-the-clock care in her final months, Makena had been in no position to disappear. And she'd known that was exactly what she had to do, when she walked away from River after his threats.

When Makena looked up, she realized that Colton had been studying her.

"What's his name?" he asked. Those three words slammed into her. They were so on point it took her back for a second.

She opened her mouth to protest the question, but Colton waved her off before she could get a word out.

"Makena, you don't have to tell me his

name. I'll leave that up to you. Just don't lie to me about him existing at all."

Well, now she really felt bad. She sat there for a long moment and contemplated her next move. Having lived alone for six months after losing her mother, barely saying a word to anyone and focusing on the basest level of survival, she now wanted to open up to someone.

She just wanted to be honest with someone and with herself for a change.

"River."

She didn't look up at Colton right then. She wouldn't be able to bear a look of pity. She didn't want him to feel sorry for her. It was her mistake. She'd made it. She'd owned it. She would've moved on a long time ago if it hadn't been for her mother's illness.

"Was he abusive? Did he lay a hand on you?" The seriousness and calmness in Colton's tone didn't convey pity at all. It sounded more like compassion and understanding. Two words that were so foreign to her when it came to her relationship with a man.

"No." She risked a glance at him. "He would've. We started off with arguments that escalated. He always took it too far. He'd say the most hurtful things meant to cut me to the quick. I didn't grow up with a father in the house. So I didn't know how abnormal that was in a relationship."

"No one should have to." There was no judgment in his voice but there was anger.

"Things escalated pretty badly, and one day when we were arguing I stomped into the bedroom. He followed and when I wouldn't stop, he grabbed my wrist like he was a vise on the tightest notch. He whirled me around so hard that the back of my head smacked against the wall. I was too prideful to let him know how much it hurt. It wasn't intentional on his part. Not that part. But he immediately balled his fist and reared it back."

Makena had to breathe slowly in order to continue. Her heart raced at hearing the words spoken aloud that she'd bottled up for so long. Panic tightened her chest.

"What did you do to stop him from hitting you?" Colton's jaw muscle clenched.

"I looked him dead in the eyes, refusing to buckle or let him know that I was afraid. And then I told him to go ahead and do it. Hit me. But I cautioned him with this. I told him that if he did throw that punch he'd better sleep with one eye open for the rest of his life because we had a fireplace with a fireplace poker and I told him that he would wake up one morning to find it buried right in between his eyes."

A small smile ghosted Colton's lips. "Good for you. I bet he thought twice about ever putting a hand on you again."

"Honestly, I don't think I could ever

hurt another human being unless my life depended on it. But I needed him to believe every word of that. And he did. That was the first and last time he raised a fist to me. But his words were worse in some ways. They cut deep and he tried to keep a tight rein on who I saw and where I went."

"Can I ask you a question?"

"Go ahead." She'd shared a lot more about her situation than she'd ever thought she would with anyone. Part of her needed to talk about it with someone. She'd never told her mom because she didn't want her to worry.

"Why did you stay?"

"My mom. She was sick for a couple of years and then she passed away." Makena paused long enough to catch her breath. She tucked her chin to her chest so he wouldn't see the tears welling in her eyes. "That's when I left him. Before that, honestly, she needed me to be stable for her. She needed someone to take care of her and she needed to stay with the same doctors. I couldn't relocate her." Makena decided not to share the rest of that story. And especially not the part where River had threatened her life if she ever left him. He seemed to catch onto the fact that she'd at the very least been thinking about leaving.

But Makena didn't want to think about that anymore, and she sure as hell didn't want to talk about herself. She'd done enough of that for one night. She picked up her coffee and took a sip before turning the tables.

Catching Colton's gaze, she asked, "How about you? Tell me about your wife."

"There isn't much to tell. Rebecca and I were best friends. She lived across the street and we grew up together. Her father is the mayor. We dated in high school and broke up to go to different colleges. Her older sister had married her high school sweetheart and the relationship fell apart in college, so Rebecca was concerned the same thing would happen to us."

"And what did you think?"

"That I was ready for a break. I looked at our relationship a lot like most people look at religion. When someone grows up in a certain church, it's all they know. Part of growing up and becoming independent is testing different waters and making certain it's the right thing for you and not just what's ingrained. You know?"

"Makes a lot of sense to me." She nodded.

"Before I committed the rest of my life to someone, I wanted to make damn sure I was making the right call and not acting out of habit. That's what the break meant to me."

"Since the two of you married, I'm

guessing you realized she was the one."

Why did that make Makena's heart hurt?

"You could say that. I guess I figured there were worse things than marrying my best friend."

Makena picked up on the fact that he hadn't described Rebecca as the love of his life or the woman he wanted to spend the rest of his life with, or said the two of them had realized they were perfect for each other.

"We got married and the twins came soon after. And then almost immediately after, she was hit by a drunk driver on the highway coming home from visiting her sister in Austin. She died instantly. I'd kept the twins home with me that day to give her a break."

"I'm so sorry, Colton."

"I rented this apartment after not really wanting to live on the ranch in our home. The place just seemed so empty without her. I go there on my days off with the twins because we still have pictures of her hanging up there and I want the twins to have some memories of growing up in a house surrounded by their mother's things."

"Being a single dad must be hard. You seem like you're doing a really great job with your boys. I bet she'd be really proud of you."

"It really means a lot to hear you say that. I'd like to think she would be proud. I want to make her proud. She deserved that." A storm brewed behind his eyes when he spoke about his wife.

"How long were the two of you married?" Makena asked, wanting to know more about his life after college.

"We got married after she told me that she was pregnant."

Was that the reason he'd said he could've done worse than marrying his best friend? Had she gotten pregnant and they'd married? Asking him seemed too personal. If he wanted her to know, he probably would've told her by now. The questions seemed off-limits even though they'd both shared more than either of them had probably set out to at the beginning of this conversation.

Despite the boost of caffeine, Makena had never felt more tired. It was probably the rain, which had settled into a steady, driving rhythm, coupled with the fact that she hadn't really slept since almost running into the pair of men she'd seen with River, not to mention she'd been clipped by an SUV. She bit back another yawn and tried to rally.

"Losing her must've been hard for you, Colton. I couldn't be sorrier that happened. You deserve so much more. You deserved a life together."

COLTON HADN'T EXPECTED to talk so much about Rebecca. Words couldn't describe how much he missed his best friend.

There was something about telling their story that eased some of the pain in his chest. He was coming up on a year without her in a few days. And even though theirs hadn't been an epic love that made his heart race every time she was near, it had been built on friendship. He could've done a lot worse.

Being with Makena had woken up his heart and stirred feelings in him that he'd thought were long since dead. In fact, he hadn't felt this way since meeting her sophomore year. He'd known something different was up the minute he'd seen Makena. Rebecca had texted him that day to see how he was doing and it was the first time he hadn't responded right away.

Rebecca had picked up on the reason. Hell, there were times when he could've sworn she knew him better than he knew himself.

Being here, with Makena, felt right on

so many levels. It eased some of the ache of losing his best friend. Not that his feelings for Makena were anything like his marriage to Rebecca. He and Rebecca were about shared history, loyalty and a promise to have each other's back until the very end.

Colton felt a lot of pride in following through on his promise. He'd had Rebecca's back. He'd always have her back. And in bringing up the twins, he was given an opportunity to prove his loyalty to his best friend every day. Those boys looked like their mother and reminded him of her in so many ways. A piece of her, a very large piece, would always be with him.

He reminded himself of the fact every day.

Right now, his focus was on making certain the residents in his county were safe and that fearful look that showed up on Makena's face every once in a while for the briefest moment subsided. She'd opened up to him about living with a verbally abusive ex. Colton had a lot of experience with domestic situations. More than he cared to. He'd seen firsthand the collateral damage from relationships that became abusive and felt boiling hot anger run through his veins.

He flexed and released his fingers to try to ease out some of the tension building in him at the thought of Makena in a similar predicament. He'd also witnessed the hold an abusive spouse could have over the other person. Men tended to be the more physically aggressive, although there were times when he saw abuse the other way around. Women tended to use verbal assaults to break a partner down. He'd seen that, too. Except that the law didn't provide for abuse that couldn't be seen.

Texas law protected against bruises and bloody noses, ignoring the fact that verbal abuse could rank right up there in damage. The mental toll was enormous. Studying Makena now and knowing what she'd been like in the past, he couldn't imagine her living like that.

"How long were you married?" he asked.

"Nine years." The shock of that sat with him for a long minute as he took another sip of fresh brew.

"Was your mother the only reason you stayed?" he asked.

"Honestly?"

He nodded.

"Yes. She got sick and couldn't seem to shake it. I took her to a doctor and then a specialist, and then another specialist. By the time they figured out what was wrong with her, she had a stroke. It was too late to save her." She ran her finger along the rim of her coffee cup.

The look of loss on Makena's face when she spoke about her mother was a gut punch. She didn't have that same look when she talked about her ex. With him, there was sometimes a flash of fear and most definitely defiance. Her chin would jut out and resolve would darken her features.

"I miss her every day," she admitted.

Since the words *I'm sorry* seemed to fall short, he set his coffee down and pushed up to standing. He took the couple of steps to the other couch and sat beside her. Taking her hand in his, he hoped to convey his sympathy for the loss of her mother.

"She's the reason that I got to go to college. She, and a very determined college counselor. It was just me and my mom for so long. She sacrificed everything for me."

"Your mother sounds like an incredible person."

"She was." Makena ducked her head down, chin to chest, and he realized she was hiding the fact that a tear had rolled down her face.

"I can imagine how difficult it was for her to bring you up alone. There are days when I feel like my butt is being kicked bringing up my boys. Without my family by my side, I don't even see how it's possible to do it. I don't know what I'd do without my tribe and their help."

"Whoever said it takes a village to bring up a child was right. We just had two people in ours and it was always just kind of us against the world. It wasn't all bad. I mean, I didn't even realize how many sacrifices my mom made for me until I was grown and had my first real job out of college. Then I started realizing how expensive things were and how much she covered. I saw what it took to get by financially. She didn't have a college education and insisted that I get one. She worked long hours to make sure that it could happen without me going into a ridiculous amount of debt. I never told her when I had to take out student loans because I wanted her to feel like she was able to do it all."

"It sounds like you gave her a remarkable gift. Again, I can only compare it to my boys but I also know that I want to give them the world just like I'm sure your mom wanted to with you. The fact that she was able to do as much as she did with very little resources and no support is nothing short of a miracle. It blows me away."

He paused long enough for her to lift her gaze up to meet his, and when it did, that jolt of electricity coursed through him.

"It's easy to see where you get your strength from now." Colton was rewarded with a smile that sent warmth spiraling through him before zeroing in on his heart.

"Colton…" Whatever Makena was about to say seemed to die on her lips.

"For what it's worth, you deserve better, with what you got from your marriage and the loss of your mother so young," he said.

She squeezed his arm in a move that was probably meant to be reassuring but sent another charge jolting through him, lighting up his senses and making him even more aware of her. This close, he breathed in her unique scent, roses in spring. The mood changed from sadness and sharing to awareness—awareness of her pulse pounding at the base of her throat, awareness of the chemistry that was impossible to ignore.

He reached up and brushed the backs of his fingers against her cheek and then her jawline. She took hold of his forearm and then pulled him closer, their gazes locked the entire time.

When she tugged him so close, their

lips were inches apart, and his tongue darted across his lips. He could only imagine how incredible she would taste. A moment of caution settled over him as his pulse skyrocketed. His caution had nothing to do with how badly he wanted to close the distance between them and everything to do with a stab of guilt. It was impossible not to feel like he was betraying Rebecca in some small measure, especially since his feelings for Makena were a runaway train.

He reminded himself that his wife was gone and had been for almost a year. It was a long time since he'd been with someone other than her, and that would mess with anyone's mind. Not to mention the fact he hadn't felt this strong an attraction to anyone. In fact, the last time he had was with the woman whose lips were inches from his.

Makena brought her hands up to touch

his face, silently urging him to close that gap.

Colton closed his eyes and breathed in her flowery scent. He leaned forward and pressed his lips to hers. Hers were delicate and soft despite the fiery and confident woman behind them.

All logic and reason flew out the window the second their mouths fused. He drove the tip of his tongue inside her mouth. She tasted like sweet coffee. Normally, he took his black. Sweet was his new favorite flavor.

Makena moved toward him and broke into the moment with a wince. She pulled back. "Sorry."

"Don't be." He wanted to offer more reassurance than that but couldn't find the right words. Either way, this was just the shot of reality that he needed before he let things get out of hand. Doing any of this with her right now was the worst of bad ideas.

They were two broken souls connecting and that was it. So why did the sentiment feel hollow? Why did his mind try to argue the opposite? Why did it insist these feelings were very real? The attraction was different? And it was still very much alive between them?

"I'm sorry if I hurt you," he finally said.

"You couldn't have. It was my fault. I got a little carried away." Her breathing was raspy, much like his own.

He'd never experienced going from zero to one hundred miles an hour from what started as a slow burn. Don't get him wrong, he'd experienced great sex. This was somehow different. The draw toward Makena was sun to earth.

Colton was certain of one thing. Sex with Makena would be mind-blowing and a game changer. With her hip in the condition it was, there was no threat it was going to happen anytime soon. That shouldn't make his chest deflate like someone had just let the air out of a balloon. He chalked it up to the lack of sex in his life and, even more than that, the lack of companionship.

This was the first time he realized how much he missed having someone to talk to when he walked in the door at night. Having the twins was amazing but one-year-olds weren't exactly known for their conversation skills.

Colton took the interruption from the hip pain as a sign he was headed down the wrong path. Granted, it didn't feel misguided, and nothing inside him wanted to stop, but doing anything to cause her more pain was out of the question.

A voice in the back of his mind picked that time to remind him of the fact he'd struck her with his vehicle. He was the reason she was in pain in the first place.

The idea that she'd been adamant about not filing a report crept into his thoughts.

As much as she'd insisted not doing so was for his benefit, he'd quickly ascertained that she didn't want her name attached to a report. Colton had already put two and two together and guessed she was hiding out from her ex. But living in a random trailer and hiding her name meant her situation was more complicated than he'd first realized. No matter what else, this was a good time to take a break and regroup.

"I'm sorry. That whole kissing thing was my fault. I don't know what came over me." Makena's cheeks flushed with embarrassment and that only poured gasoline onto the fire of attraction burning in him.

"Last I checked, I was a pretty willing participant." He winked and she smiled. He hadn't meant to make her feel bad by regrouping. In fact, the last thing he wanted to do was add to her stress. Based on what she'd shared so far, her marriage had done very little to lift her up and inspire confidence.

Was it wrong that he wanted to be the person who did that for her?

Chapter Six

Embarrassment didn't begin to cover the emotion Makena should be feeling after practically throwing herself at Colton. It was impossible to regret her actions, though. She hadn't been so thoroughly kissed by any man in her entire life. That was a sad statement considering she'd been married, but wow, Colton could kiss. He brought parts of her to life that had been dormant for so long she'd forgotten they existed.

She wanted to chalk up the thrill of the kiss to the fact that it had been more than a decade in the making, but that would sell it short. He'd barely dipped the tip of his tongue in her mouth and yet it was the most erotic kiss she'd ever experienced. She could only imagine what it would feel like to take the next step with him.

And since those thoughts were about as productive as spending all her paycheck on a pair of shoes, she shelved them. For now, at least.

Makena blew out an awkward breath. Yes, dwelling on their attraction was off the table, because not only was it futile, but there was no way she could compete with a ghost. Colton had said so himself. He'd married his best friend. His beloved wife had died shortly after giving birth to their twins and making a family.

Despite the fact that he hadn't described his relationship with his wife as anything other than a deep friendship, it would be impossible to stack up to that level of love.

Colton's gaze darted to his coffee cup. "Mine's empty. How are you on a refill?"

"I'm good. I think I've had enough." She bit back a yawn. "If it's okay, I'd like to just curl up here and rest my eyes for a few minutes."

"Make yourself at home." Colton stood. The couch felt immediately cold to her, after his warmth from a few moments ago. He scooped up his coffee mug and headed toward the kitchen. She could've sworn she heard him mumble phrases like "another time and place and things might be different," and "bad timing." She couldn't be certain. It might've just been wishful thinking on her part to believe there was something real going on between them.

An awkward laugh escaped. She'd never been the type to latch onto someone, but then this wasn't just anyone. Was she seriously that lonely?

This was Colton O'Connor and they

shared history. And based on the enthu-
siasm in his kiss, an attraction that hadn't
completely run its course.

Makena counted herself lucky that embarrassment couldn't kill a person. Actually, maybe it wasn't embarrassment she
felt. Maybe it was that strong attraction
that caused her cheeks to heat. When she
really thought about it, she hadn't done
anything to be embarrassed about.

The past six months, being alone, had
done a number on her mindset. That was
certain. But it hadn't knocked her out.
And it wouldn't. She would get through
this, rebound and pick her life up again.
A life that seemed a little bit colder now
that she'd been around warmth again.

Makena figured it was too much to
hope that she'd find her feet rooted in the
real world again. And real world started
with a few basics. "Hey, Colton. Any
chance you have a spare toothbrush and
a washcloth I could use?"

Her clothes were in the dryer, so she might as well go all in wishing for a real shower rather than a bowl of warm soapy water by the river like she'd done the past few days at the RV.

"Like I said, make yourself at home." He tilted his head toward the hallway where he'd disappeared earlier to bring her the robe. "You'll find a full bathroom in there. Spare toothbrushes are still in the wrappers in the cabinet."

With some effort, Makena was able to stand. Colton turned around and a look of shock stamped his features.

"Hold on there. I can help you get to the bathroom."

"It still hurts, I'm not going to lie. But it's not as bad as it was an hour ago. I'd like to see if I can make it myself." She wasn't exactly fast and couldn't outrun an ant, but she was proud of the fact that she made it to the bathroom on her own. She closed the toilet seat, folded a towel and paused a moment to catch her breath. It was progress and she'd take it.

As she sat in the bathroom waiting for the pain in her hip to subside, she couldn't help but inhale a deep breath, filling her senses with Colton's scent. The bathrobe she wore smelled like him, all campfire and outdoors and spice. It was masculine and everything she'd remembered about sitting next to him in biology lab. His scent was all over the robe.

She needed to get her head on straight and refocus. Thinking much more about Colton and how amazing and masculine he smelled wasn't going to help her come up with a plan of what to do next.

It would probably be best for all concerned if she could put Colton out of her head altogether. She appreciated his help, though.

Taking another deep breath, Makena reached over and turned on the water. Using the one-step-at-a-time method, she peeled off the bathrobe and then took baby steps until she was standing in the massive shower. She had no idea what materials actually were used, but the entire shower enclosure looked like it was made of white marble. There were two showerheads. The place was obviously meant for a couple to be able to shower together. However, a half dozen people would fit inside there at the very least.

Now that really made Makena laugh. Images of single father and town sheriff Colton in a wild shower party with a half dozen people didn't really fit well together.

They tickled her anyway.

And maybe she was just that giddy. Exhaustion started wearing her thin, and her nerves, nerves that had been fried for a solid year and really longer than that if she thought back, eased with being around Colton.

The soap might smell clean and a little spicy, but it was the warm water that got her. Amazing didn't begin to cover it. She showered as quickly as possible, though, not wanting to keep too much pressure on that hip. Her left side bit back with pain any time she put pressure on it.

After toweling off and slipping back into the robe, she brushed her teeth. She had a toothbrush at the RV, in the small bag of shower supplies she kept with her at all times while on the move. But this was a luxury. It was crazy how the simple things felt so good after being deprived. Simple things like a real shower and a real bathroom.

Speaking of which, the cup of coffee that she'd had a little while ago had been in a league of its own.

Makena reminded herself not to get too comfortable here. It was dangerous to let her guard down or stick around longer than absolutely necessary. Being in one place for too long was a hazard, made more so by the fact her identity could be so easily revealed by Colton.

She tightened the tie on the bathrobe before exiting the bathroom and making her way back into the living room. She might move slow, but this was progress. If she could rest that hip for a couple of hours and let the worst of the storm pass, she could get back to the RV and then… go where?

Thinking about her next step was her new priority. She'd been so focused on surviving one hour at a time that she'd forgotten there was a big picture—an end game that had her collecting evidence against her ex. Time had run out for her in Katy Gulch.

Inside the living room, Colton was in mission control mode. He was so deep in thought with what was going on and talking into his radio that he didn't even seem to hear her when she walked into the room.

Rather than disturb him, she moved as stealthily as possible, reclaiming her spot opposite him on the couch. He glanced up and another shot of warmth rocketed through her body, settling low in her stomach. Colton's deep, masculine voice spoke in hushed tones as she curled up on her side on the sofa. He almost immediately shifted the laptop off his lap and grabbed the blanket draped on the back of the sofa.

He walked over and placed it over her before offering her an extra throw pillow. She took it, laid her head on it and closed her eyes.

With all the stress that had been building the six months and especially in the past couple of days since she thought she'd seen River's associates, there was no way she could sleep.

Resting her eyes felt good. That was the last thought she had before she must've passed out.

Makena woke with a start. She immediately pushed up to sit and glanced around, trying to get her bearings. Her left hip screamed at her with movement, so she eased pressure from it, shifting to the right side instead.

Daylight streamed through the large windows in the loft-style apartment. She rubbed blurry eyes and yawned.

Looking around, she searched for any signs of Colton as the memory of last night became more focused. She strained to listen for him and was pretty sure she heard the shower going in the other room. The image of a naked, muscled Colton standing in the same shower she'd showered in just a few hours ago probably wasn't the best start to her morning. Or it was. Depending on how she looked at it. Makena chuckled nervously.

The events from the past twelve hours or so came back to her, bringing down her mood. She opened up the robe to examine her hip on the left side. Sure enough, a bruise the size of a bowling ball stared back at her. Pain had reminded her it was there before she'd even looked.

Movement hurt. She sucked in a breath and pushed past the soreness and pain as she closed her robe and stood. Then she remembered that Colton had some of the best coffee she'd ever tasted. Since he'd instructed her to make herself at home, she figured he wouldn't mind if she made a cup.

Her stomach growled despite the sandwich, apple and soup he'd given her. She glanced at the clock. That had been a solid ten hours ago. How had she slept so long?

Makena hadn't had that much sleep at one time in the past year. Of that she was certain. She cautioned herself against getting too comfortable around Colton. She'd already let way too much slip about her personal life, not that it hadn't felt good to finally open up to someone she trusted and talk about her mother and other parts of her life. It had. But it was also dangerous.

A part of her wanted to resurface just to see if River had let his anger toward her go by now. If he'd let *her* go by now. Being on the run, hiding out, had always made her feel like she'd done something wrong, not the other way around.

Standing up to fight a Dallas police officer who ran in a circle just like him could wreak complete havoc on her life, so she had erred on the side of caution.

But should she start over now, after she'd found Colton again? There was something almost thrilling about seeing him, about finding a piece of herself that had been alive before she'd lost her mother...before River.

If Makena was being completely honest with herself, she could admit that part of her disappearing act had to do with wanting to shut out the world after losing her mother. She'd succumbed to grief and allowed fear to override rational thought.

But where to start over? Dallas was out. Houston was a couple hours' drive away. Maybe she could make a life there? Get back to teaching music. It was worth a shot.

Living like she had been over the past few months, although necessary, wasn't really being alive.

Makena saw a coffee machine sitting on a countertop. It was easy to spot in the neat kitchen. There were drawers next to it and so she went ahead and made the wild assumption that she'd find coffee in one of them.

She didn't. But she did find some in the cupboard above. It was the pod kind. She helped herself to one that said Regular Coffee and placed it in the fancy-looking steel machine. She glanced to the side and saw a plastic carafe already filled with water.

There was only one button, so that was easy. The round metal button made the machine come to life. It was then that she realized she hadn't put a coffee cup underneath the spout.

"Oh no. Where are you?" She opened a couple of cupboards until she found the one that housed the mugs. She grabbed one and placed it under the spout just in time for the first droplets of brown liquid to sputter out. "Good save." She mumbled the words out loud and, for the second time since opening her eyes, chuckled.

Her lighter mood had everything to do with being around Colton again. The kiss they'd shared had left the memory of his taste on her lips. And even though their relationship couldn't go anywhere, the attraction between them was a nice change of pace from what she usually felt around men. After being with River, she'd become uneasy interacting with the opposite sex.

Makena slowly made her way to the fridge. Quick movement hurt. Walking hurt. But she was doing it and was certain she could push through the pain.

In the fridge, she found cups of her favorite thing in the world, vanilla yogurt. She took one and managed to find a spoon. She polished it off before the coffee could stop dripping.

The carton of eggs was tempting, but she needed to take it easy on the hip. Standing in front of the stove was probably not the best idea. The yogurt would hold her over until she could rest enough to gather the energy to find something else to eat or cook.

Cup of coffee in hand, she slowly made her way to one of the chairs at the granite island. It would be too much to ask for sugar and cream at this hour, especially with the amount of pain she was in. She hadn't asked for ibuprofen last night, not wanting to mask her injury. Today, however, she realized the injury was superficial and she would ask for a couple of pain relievers once Colton returned from the shower.

Speaking of which, she was pretty certain the water spigot had been turned off for a while now.

Nothing could have quite prepared her for the sight of Colton O'Connor when he waltzed into the room wearing nothing but a towel. The white cloth was wrapped around lean hips and tucked into one side.

"Good morning." The low timbre of his voice traveled all over her body, bringing a ripple of awareness.

"Morning to you." She diverted her gaze from the tiny droplets of water rolling down his muscled chest.

"I see you managed to find a cup of coffee. It's good to see you up and around. How's that hip today?" His smile—a show of perfectly straight, white teeth—made him devastatingly hot.

"It's better. I managed the coffee minus the cream." She decided it was best to redirect the conversation away from her injury. "This coffee is amazing straight out of the pot. Or whatever that thing is." She motioned toward the stainless-steel appliance.

Colton's eyebrow shot up and a small smile crossed his lips—lips she had no business staring at, but they were a distraction all the same.

"You want cream and sugar?"

"It's really no big deal." She'd barely finished her protest when Colton moved over to the fridge and came back with cream that he set on the counter in front of her. He located sugar next and tossed a few packets in her direction.

She thanked him.

"You seemed pretty busy last night. Is everyone okay?" she asked.

"The storm was all bark and no bite thankfully. Roads were messy, but folks respected Mother Nature and she backed off without any casualties."

"That's lucky," she said.

"There were a few close calls with stranded vehicles. Nothing I could get to, but my deputies could."

"That's a relief." She took a sip of coffee and groaned. "This is so good."

He shot her a look before shaking his head. "That's a nice sound. But not one I need in my head all day and especially not after…never mind."

The words on the tip of his tongue had to be *that kiss.* She'd thought the same thing when she saw him half-naked in the kitchen.

"I can't remember the last time I slept as well as I did last night." She stretched her arms out.

"If you slept that well on the couch, imagine what it would be like in a real bed." He seemed to hear those words as they came out and shot her a look that said he wanted to reel them back in.

The image that had popped into her thoughts was one of her in bed with him. Considering he still stood there in a towel, she needed to wipe all those thoughts from her head.

Seeing him again was making a difference in her mood and her outlook. Somewhere in the past six months after losing her mother, she'd given up a little bit on life. Looking back, she could see that so clearly now.

This morning, she felt a new lease on life and was ready to start making plans for a future. She hadn't felt like she would have one, in so long.

She took another sip of coffee. "I know that I said last night was the best cup of coffee I'd had in a long time, but this beats it."

He practically beamed with pride. "Are you hungry?"

"I already helped myself to yogurt. I hope that's okay."

"Of course it is. I make a pretty mean spinach omelet if you're game."

The man was the definition of hotness. He cared about others, hence his job as sheriff. And now he decided to tell her that he could cook?

"You're not playing fair," she teased. "I really don't want you to go to any trouble."

"If it makes you feel any better, I plan to make some for myself. No bacon, though. I'm out."

"Well, in that case, forget it. What kind of house runs out of bacon?" She laughed at her own joke and was relieved when he did, too. It was nice to be around someone who was so easy to be with. Conversation was light. This was exactly what she remembered about biology lab and why she'd been so attracted to him all those years ago. Sure, he was basically billboard material on the outside, with those features she could stare at all day. But how many people did she know who were good-looking on the outside and empty shells on the inside? A conversation with a ten on the outside and a three on substance made her want to fall asleep thinking about it.

Physical attraction was nice. It was one thing. It was important. But she'd learned a long time ago that someone's intelligence, sense of humor and wit could sway their looks one way or the other for her.

On a scale of one to ten, Colton was a thirty-five in every area.

Chapter Seven

Colton whipped up a pair of omelets and threw a couple slices of bread into the toaster while Makena finished up her cup of coffee at the granite island.

"Is there any chance I can have some pain reliever?" she asked.

"I have a bottle right here." He moved to the cabinet at the end of the counter. Medicine was kept on the top shelf even though his sons had only just taken their first steps recently. "Ibuprofen okay?"

"It's the only thing I take and that's rare."

"Same here." He grabbed a couple of tablets and then put a plate of food in front of her. "You probably want to eat that first. Ibuprofen on an empty stomach is not good."

She nodded and smiled at the plate. Tension still tightened the muscles of her face but sometime in the past twelve hours they'd been together, she'd relaxed just a bit. Given her history with men, it was wonderful that she could be this comfortable around him so quickly, and Colton let his chest fill with pride at that, although her ease was tentative, as he could tell from her eyes.

"Are you serious about these eggs?" She made a show of appreciating them after taking another bite.

Colton laughed. He realized it had been a really long time since he'd laughed this much. The roller coaster he'd been on since losing Rebecca and then his father had been awful to say the least.

To say that Colton hadn't had a whole lot to smile about recently was a lot like saying The New Texas Giant was just a roller coaster.

The exception was his twin boys. When he was with them, he did his level best to set everything else aside and just be with them. He might only have an hour or so to play with them before nighttime routine kicked in, but he treasured every moment of it. The last year had taught him that kids grew up way too fast.

"I'm glad you like the eggs."

"*Like* is too weak a word for how I feel about this omelet." Her words broke into more of that thick, heavy fog that had filled his chest for too long.

"The roads are clearing up. After you eat, I should make a few rounds."

"Can you give me a ride to the RV?" she asked.

"Happy to oblige," he teased. "I just need to get dressed."

Her cheeks flushed and he wondered if it had anything to do with the fact that he was still in a towel. A rumble of a laugh started inside his chest and rolled out. "I just realized that I'm walking about like I don't have company. Pardon me. I'll just go get dressed now."

"Well, it hasn't exactly been hard on the eyes." Now it was her turn to burst out laughing. "I can't believe I just said that out loud."

He excused himself and headed into his bedroom, where he threw on a pair of boxers, jeans and a dark, collared button-down shirt. He pulled his belt from the safe and clipped it on. It held his badge and gun.

Colton located one of his navy wind-breakers that had the word *SHERIFF* written in bright, bold letters down the left sleeve. He finger-combed his hair and was ready to go. Walking out into the living room and seeing Makena still sitting there in his robe was a punch to the chest.

"I'll go and grab your clothes from the dryer." His offer was met with a smile.

"I can go with you. Or you could just point me in a direction. I think I can find my way around," she said.

"Down the hall. Open the door in the bathroom. You probably thought it was a closet, but it's actually a laundry room."

"That's really convenient." She tightened her grip on her robe and disappeared down the hallway.

He was relieved to see that her hip seemed in better condition today. She was barely walking with a limp. Even so, he wondered if he could talk her into making a trip to the ER for an X-ray.

Ten minutes later, she emerged from the hallway. She'd brushed her hair and dressed in the jeans and blouse she'd had on yesterday. "Ready?"

"Are the pain pills kicking in yet?" he asked.

"It's actually much better. I mean, I

have a pretty big bruise, but overall, I'm in good shape. The ibuprofen is already helping. I won't be riding any bucking broncos in the next few days, but it'll heal up fine."

"I like the fact that you're walking more easily, but I would feel a whole lot better if we stopped off at the county hospital to get it checked out. The roads are clear on that route." He hoped she'd listen to reason.

She opened her mouth to protest, but he put his hand up to stop her.

"Hear me out. You won't have to pay for the cost of the X-ray. It's the least I can do considering the fact that I hit you."

"Technically, I ran out in front of your car and you didn't have enough time to stop. You also couldn't see me because of the rain. So, technically, I hit you."

Well, Colton really did laugh out loud now. That was a new one and he thought he'd heard just about every line imaginable in his profession. He couldn't help himself, and chuckled again. It was a sign she was winning him over, and he didn't normally give away his tells.

"I'm glad you're laughing, because you could be writing me up right now or arresting me for striking an official vehicle. Does that count as striking an officer?" She seemed pretty pleased with that last comment.

"All right. You got me. I laughed. It was funny. But what wouldn't be funny is if there's something seriously wrong with your hip and it got worse because we didn't get it checked out." Was it him or had he just turned into his old man? He could've sworn he'd heard those same words coming out of Finn O'Connor's mouth for most of Colton's life. His dad was great at coaxing others to get checked out. He didn't seem to think he fell into the same category.

And it was only recently that Colton and his brothers had found out his father had been dealing with a health issue that he'd kept quiet about until his death.

"Don't you think we would know by now? Plus, what's the worst it could be? A hairline fracture? I had one of those in my wrist in eighth grade PE. It's an incident I don't talk about because it highlights my general inability to perform athletics of any kind. But there wasn't much they could do with it except wrap it and put it in a sling. It wasn't like I needed a cast. I'm sure my hip falls into the same category. I need to rest. I need to take it easy. Other than that, I think I'm good to go."

What she said made a whole lot of sense, and Colton knew in the back of his mind she was right on some level. The thought of dropping her off at the RV to fend for herself after witnessing the way she'd gobbled down food last night and cleaned her plate this morning wasn't something he could stomach doing.

He wanted to help her, but he didn't want to hurt her pride. He needed to be tactful. "Since you're going to be resting for a few days anyway, why not do it here?"

The question surprised even him. But it was the logical thing to do. He had plenty of room here. He could sleep on the sofa. He'd done that countless times before, unable and unwilling to face an empty bedroom.

"That's a really kind offer. Maybe under different circumstances I could take you up on it..."

"I didn't want to have to pull this card out, but since you mentioned it, you're leaving me no choice." He caught hold of her gaze and tried his level best not to give himself away by laughing. "If you don't stay here and let me help you heal, I might be forced to handcuff you."

He mustered up his most serious expression.

Makena's jaw nearly dropped to the floor, and a twinge of guilt struck him at tricking her.

"That's blackmail. You wouldn't do that to me. Would you?" Her question was uncertain and he suspected she'd figured out his prank.

"I don't know." He shrugged. "Is it working?"

She walked straight toward him with her slight limp on the left side and gave him a playful jab on the shoulder. "That wasn't funny."

"Actually, I thought it was ingenious of me." Seeing the lighter side of Makena and her quick wit reminded him of why he'd been willing to walk away from the relationship he'd known his entire life, for someone he'd met in biology lab.

Deep down, behind those sad and suspicious eyes, she was still in there. Still the playful, intelligent, perceptive woman he'd fallen for.

"I'm probably going to regret this, but I'll think about staying here until I get better. Maybe just a day or two. But..."

"Why is there always a *but*?" He rubbed the day-old scruff on his chin.

"But I sleep on the couch. You only have two bedrooms here. One is yours and the other has two cribs in it. The door was open on the way to the bathroom. I couldn't help but notice," she said in her defense.

"Yes, you can stay here. Thank you for asking. And who sleeps on the couch is up for debate. We'll figure out a fair way to decide." There was no way he was going to let her curl up on the sofa when he had a king-size bed in the other room. Most of the time, he nodded off with a laptop open next to him and a phone in his hand anyway. It was easier than facing an empty bed on his own.

"And hey, thanks for considering my proposal," he added.

Colton appreciated how difficult her situation must be for her to feel the need to hide in a random stranger's RV, and he appreciated the confidence she put in him by staying with him last night.

In the ultimate display of trust, she'd fallen deeply asleep.

She didn't speak, but he could see the impact of his words. Sometimes, silence said more than a thousand words ever could.

Colton put his hand on the small of Makena's back as he escorted her to the elevator. Emotions seemed to be getting the best of her, because she'd gotten all serious and quiet on him again. The lighter mood was gone and he wondered if it had something to do with what he'd said or the simple fact they were going back to the RV where she'd been staying.

There were so many unanswered questions bubbling up in his mind about Makena and her need to hide. Abusive exes he understood. But she'd been in hiding for months, and he wondered how much of it had to do with losing her mother. He knew firsthand what it was like to have a close bond with a parent who died. Colton and his siblings were still reeling from the loss of their father. Worsened by the fact none of them could solve the decades-old mystery about their only sister's abduction from her bedroom window.

Frustration was building with each passing day, along with the realization their father had gone to his deathbed never knowing what had happened to Caroline. Plus, there was the whole mess of Caroline's kidnapping being dredged up in the news ever since there'd been a kidnapping attempt in town a couple of months ago.

Renee Smith, now Renee O'Connor after marrying his brother Cash, had moved to Katy Gulch with her six-month-old daughter, Abby, in order to start a new life. Her past had come with her and it was a haunting reminder of what could happen when a relationship went sour.

Renee's ex had followed her to Katy Gulch unbeknownst to her and tried to take away the one thing she loved most, in order to frighten her into coming home.

Was Makena in the same boat?

At least in Makena's case, she knew what she was dealing with. Renee had been caught off guard because her ex had cheated on her and was having a child with a coworker before deciding no one else could have Renee. That was pretty much where the comparisons between the two ended.

He'd brought up a good point, though. Colton wanted to know more about Makena's ex so he could determine just how much danger she might be in.

The fact she'd left the man a year ago stuck in Colton's craw. The way he'd found her and discovered how she'd been living made him think that she'd either run out of money or couldn't get to hers.

But then, he didn't know many people who could go a year without working and survive. Colton may have come from one of the wealthiest cattle ranching families in Texas, but all the O'Connors had grown up with their feet on the ground and their heads out of the clouds. Each one was determined to make a mark on this life and not rely on the good graces of their family to earn a living despite loving the land and the family business.

Colton helped Makena into the passenger seat, where she buckled herself in. The drive to Mrs. Dillon's place was short. Colton checked in with Gert on the way and the rest of the car ride he spent mulling over what he already knew.

He hoped Makena was seriously considering his offer to let her stay at his apartment. He couldn't think of a safer place for her to heal. It dawned on him that he hadn't even asked her if she liked children. He just assumed she did.

That was one of the funny things about becoming a parent: he was guilty of thinking that everyone loved kids. Growing up in Katy Gulch didn't help, because most people were kind to children in his hometown.

Colton had to stop a couple of times to clear the road of debris. So far, it was looking like Katy Gulch had been spared the storm's fury.

Gert had reported in several times last night and first thing this morning to let him know that very few people had lost power. Neighbors were pitching in to make sure food didn't spoil and people had what they needed. It was one of the many reasons Colton couldn't imagine bringing up his boys in any other place.

The twins were fifth-generation O'Connors, but whether or not they took up ranching would be up to them. Both seemed happiest when they were outdoors. Colton prayed he could give them half the childhood he'd been fortunate to have. He and his brothers had had the best. Of course, they'd also had their fair share of squabbles over the years.

Garrett and Cash seemed to rub each other the wrong way from just about the day Garrett was born. Make no mistake about it, though. Either one would be there for the other in a snap. Help needed? No questions asked.

Was it strange that Colton wished the same for Makena? He wished she could experience being part of a big family. It sounded like since losing her mother, she'd lost all the family she had. He couldn't even imagine what that would be like.

She'd remained quiet on the way over. They were getting close to Mrs. Dillon's and the river.

"Everything all right over there?" he asked her.

"Yeah, I'm good." The words were spoken with no conviction.

From the way she drawled out those three words, he could tell she was deep in thought. Her voice always had that sound when she was deep in concentration. He'd once accidentally interrupted her studying and heard that same sound.

He'd given her a lot to think about. To him, it was a no-brainer decision. Knowing Makena, she wouldn't want to live off him for free even for a few days.

It occurred to him that he was momentarily without a sitter. He wasn't even sure if she was up for the job, considering her left hip. She was walking better today, but she would know better than anyone else if she'd be able to keep up with the boys.

For the time being, it was a lot of bending over and letting them hold your fingers while they practiced walking. They also had swings and walkers and every other kid device his mother could think to buy for them.

He could put gates up to make it easier for her. More and more, he liked the idea. It would give her some pocket money and a legitimate place to stay. She wouldn't have to feel like she was imposing, if she took a short-term job with him just until he found someone permanent.

"How are you with children?"

"They seem to like me. I have been a music teacher in an elementary school. I don't know about little-littles. I don't have much experience with anyone younger than the age of five. But I do seem to be popular with eight-year-olds." Hearing her voice light up when she talked about her career warmed his heart. "Why?"

"It's just an idea. I already told you my babysitter had an emergency in Austin and had to quit. I also mentioned having my boys with my mom at the ranch isn't ideal for anything less than short-term. We have a lot going on in our family right now with our father passing recently. I was just wondering if you'd be interested in helping me out of a pinch. Would you consider taking care of the boys until I could find someone else full-time?"

He gripped the steering wheel until his knuckles went white, as he waited for an answer.

"When would you need me to start?"

Was she seriously considering this? Before she could change her mind, he added, "Now would be good. My mom can hang on for a couple more days if needed."

"Can you give me a few hours to think about it?"

"Take all the time you need, Makena. I don't have any interviews set up just yet. Mom is on board with helping for a few days. I'm just trying to lighten her load."

"Okay." She nodded, giving him the impression that she liked the idea. "It's definitely something to think about. Maybe I could just meet the boys and see if they even like me."

"That's a good first step. I'm sure they will, though. They're easygoing babies. It might be good for you to see if that age scares you, without the pressure of signing on for a commitment." He liked the idea of taking some of the burden off his mother, considering everything she was going through. And the thought of Makena sticking around for a while.

"I've been so focused on my situation that I haven't considered what your family must be going through," she said. The conversation ended when Colton parked at Mrs. Dillon's house.

Makena had opened the passenger door and was out of the vehicle before Colton could get around to help her. "I just want to pick up the few things I always have with me."

As she walked toward the RV, a bad feeling gripped him.

He glanced around, unable to find the source that was causing the hairs on the back of his neck to tingle.

Why did it feel like they were walking into a trap?

Chapter Eight

The silver bullet–style RV sat on a parking pad behind the farmhouse and near the river. Makena had placed a foot on the step leading into the RV when she heard Colton's voice in the background, warning her. She craned her neck to get a good look at him.

"Stop." That one word was spoken with the kind of authority she'd never heard from him before. It was the same commanding cop voice she'd heard from River.

Colton locked gazes with her. "Take your hand off the handle slowly. Don't put any pressure on the latch. And then freeze."

Makena stood fixed to the spot as a chill raced up her spine at the forceful tone. The "cop voice" brought back a flood of bad memories.

Would it always remind her of River when she heard Colton talk like that? Even a simple friendship, let alone anything more, was out of the question if her body started trembling when she heard him give an order.

She also knew better than to argue with him. He'd obviously seen something and was warning her.

"Stay right where you are. Don't move." He was by her side in a matter of seconds.

Makena's heart hammered against her rib cage, beating out a staccato rhythm. Panic squeezed her chest, making inhaling air hurt.

"Stay steady. Don't shift your weight."

Colton dropped down to all fours. In that moment, she knew exactly what he was looking for.

A bomb.

Sweat beaded on her forehead and rolled down her cheek. She focused on her breathing and willed herself not to flinch. She reminded herself to slowly breathe in and out. Her hands felt cold and clammy.

Although she couldn't exactly say she'd been living the past six months, she didn't want to die, either. And especially not here.

Her mouth tried to open but her throat was dry, and she couldn't seem to form words. Fear was replaced with anger. Anger at the fact that by hiding, she'd allowed River to run her life all these months. She'd been miserable and lonely, and had nearly starved because of him. But she'd survived. Now there'd be no going back.

Makena decided by sheer force of will that she would live. No matter what else happened, she would make it through this. It was the only choice she would allow herself to consider.

"There's a device strapped to the bottom of this step. Stay as still as you possibly can. We're going to get through this." Colton pushed up to standing and quickly scanned the area. Based on the expression on his face, which was calmer than she felt, she knew the situation was bad. He was too calm.

From the few action movies she'd seen, it seemed like if she moved, she'd be blown sky-high. She was afraid even to ask, because a slight shift in her weight, no matter how subconsciously she did it, would scatter her into a thousand tiny bits. More of that ice in her veins was replaced by fire.

River didn't get to do this. If anything happened to her, she needed Colton to know who was responsible. "My ex." She slowly exhaled, careful not to move so much as an inch.

"His name is River Myers. He works at the Dallas Police Department as an officer. He's the reason I've been on the run for the past six months. He has threatened me on numerous occasions. I walked away from a man who is armed and dangerous. He's calculating. He'll destroy me if he finds me before I locate evidence against him," she said in a voice as steady as the current in the river next to them.

"Don't you give up on me now. You're going to be fine. But the clock is ticking. I have no idea how much explosive is here and we're running out of options."

With that, he literally dove on top of her, knocking her off the step and covering her with his own body. When a blast didn't immediately occur, he said, "Let's get out of here."

With one arm hooked under her armpit, he scrambled toward a tree near the riverbank. He rounded the tree, placing it in between them and the RV. He hauled her back against his chest. He leaned back against the tree and dropped down, wrapping his arms around her.

Not two seconds later, an explosion sounded.

Her first thought was that she was thankful for Colton. If he hadn't been there, she'd be dead. Her brain couldn't process that information. It was going to take a while for that to sink in. Her second thought, as Colton's arms hugged her in a protective embrace, was that everything she'd owned in the past few months was gone.

The guitar her mother had given her had been blown to smithereens. The few clothes she had were gone along with it. It wasn't much but it was all she owned in the world.

A few tears of loss leaked out of her eyes. She sniffed them back, reminding herself this could've been a whole lot worse. It was hard to imagine, though. She had so little left from her mother.

She brought her right hand up, tracing the rose necklace with her fingers. Thankfully, she had at least one thing left from her mother.

A little voice in the back of her head pointed out that she had someone in her corner for the first time in a very long time. It wasn't the security of her mother's guitar or the few articles of clothing that meant something to her. But she had the necklace and she had Colton.

She would have to rebuild from there.

And then another thought struck. She was in danger. Real danger. Colton had a young family, and because of her, his twins had been almost orphaned. She'd never been more certain of the fact that she couldn't accept his help any longer.

Moving forward, she planned to ask him for a loan, some kind of cover identity and a ticket out of town. She'd been crazy to stay in Texas. It was only a matter of time before River and his buddies would find her there. She'd adopted the hiding-in-plain-sight strategy and it had backfired big time.

Staying in the country was no longer an option. Since Mexico bordered Texas, she could slip across the border and make a new life. Maybe she could get down to one of the resorts and work in a kitchen or someplace where she'd be hidden from view.

A ringing noise in her ear covered the sound of Colton's voice. The only reason she realized he was talking at all was because she felt his chest vibrate against her back. The blast had been deafening. And at least temporarily, she'd lost hearing. Bits of metal had blown past her and the last thing she'd heard was the bomb detonate.

Everything felt like it was moving in slow motion. It was like time had stopped and everything around her moved in those old-fashioned movie frames and some mastermind stood behind a curtain clicking slides.

When the last of the debris seemed to have flown past and everything was still, Colton scooted out from underneath her and whirled around to check the damage.

Her heart went out to the owner, the sweet woman who'd just lost a remnant from her past.

Makena balled her fists and slammed them into the unforgiving earth in frustration.

Colton had disappeared from view. She rolled around onto all fours to see for herself. The door had been blown completely off its hinges. Many of the contents had gone flying. The RV was on fire. Colton had raced to his sport utility and returned with a fire extinguisher before she was able to get to her feet.

River hadn't just sent a potent message. His intention had been to kill her. All those times he'd threatened her came racing back. And so did the memory of the pair of men she'd seen the other day.

WITHIN THE HOUR, Colton had cordoned off the crime scene. A few of his deputies arrived on-site to aid in the investigation. There was no need to call in a bomb expert. The one that had caused the kind of damage the RV had sustained was a simple job. One that anyone could've logged onto the internet and bought materials to make.

Hell, any person old enough to know how to use a phone and have access to a credit card could grab the materials used here. The bomb was crude but would've done the job of killing Makena if he hadn't been there.

A ringing noise still sounded in Colton's ears, but his hearing was coming back at least. People didn't have to shout at him anymore for him to hear what they were saying.

Deputy Fletcher walked over. He had on gloves. His palm was out, and a key chain was on top. It was a classic hotel style, with the words *Home sweet home* inscribed on the black plastic.

"What's this?" Colton asked his deputy.

Fletcher shrugged. "Found it about fifteen feet from the RV."

"Let's check with Makena to see if she recognizes it." He led Fletcher over to the spot where she was being examined by EMT Samantha Rodriguez. There were no visible signs of bleeding, so she'd been spared being impaled by debris. Colton, on the other hand, hadn't been so lucky. He'd taken a nick to his shoulder, and he was holding a T-shirt pressed to the wound to stem the bleeding.

Samantha's partner, Oliver Matthew, had tried to get Colton to stop long enough for treatment, but he had a crime scene to manage and wouldn't take any chance that evidence could end up trampled on.

"Does this look familiar to you?" he asked Makena, pointing toward the key chain on Fletcher's palm.

She gasped.

"I bought one just like that for River after moving in together. He kept losing his key, so I ordered a key chain for him. That looks exactly like the one I bought," she stated.

"Bag it and see if you can lift a print," he said to Fletcher.

"Yes, sir." Fletcher turned and walked toward his service vehicle after thanking Makena for her confirmation.

Although any Joe Schmo could make

this bomb, Colton had zeroed in on one name: River Myers. And now he might have proof. Colton was a little too familiar with the law enforcement statistics. Police officers battered their spouses in shockingly high numbers. The stress of the job was partly to blame and the reason why Colton, as a law enforcement leader, went to great lengths to offer programs and resources to help combat a pervasive issue with his deputies and employees. He saw it as his responsibility to ensure the mental and physical fitness of the men and women who served under him.

However, he could only keep an eye on his employees and do his level best to ensure they had plenty of tools to manage the stress that came with a career like theirs. He couldn't force them to take advantage of a program. An old saying came to mind: "You can lead a horse to water but you can't make it drink."

One of the advantages of running a smaller department like his office came in the form of being able to be up-front and personal with each one of his employees. A large department like Dallas wouldn't have that same benefit. Running an organization that large presented challenges.

In no way, shape or form was Colton condoning or justifying what a cop under duress might do. He held his people to the highest standards. Part of the reason why he was so selective in the hiring process. In a bigger setup, it would be easier to slip through the cracks.

When the site had been secured and medical attention given, he made his way back to Makena. Samantha turned to him.

"Her hearing should return to normal in a few days. Other than that, she was very lucky."

The last word Colton would use to describe Makena was *lucky*. Bad things happened to good people sometimes. But he understood what Samantha meant. The situation could've been a whole lot worse, with neither one of them walking away from it.

They'd also been fortunate that the pressure on the step had set off a timer and not a detonator. Those critical fifteen seconds had saved both of their lives.

"I'm so sorry, Colton. I should've known something like this would happen." Makena's pale blue eyes were wide. Fear flashed across them for a moment, followed by anger and determination. Two emotions that could get her in trouble.

"You know this isn't your fault." He needed to reassure her of the fact. He thanked Samantha.

The EMT folded her arms, put her feet in an athletic stance and shot him a death glare. "You are going to let me check out that shoulder now. Right?"

Samantha knew him well enough to realize he would put up a fight. Colton always made sure everyone around him was okay first.

"I'm standing here right now, aren't I?"

"Good." She didn't bother to hide the shock in her voice. She bent down to her medical bag and ordered him to take off his shirt, which he did.

"This is the only injury I sustained other than the ears, just like Makena."

Samantha stood up and made quick work tending to the cut in his shoulder. Within minutes, she'd cleaned the wound, applied antibiotic ointment and patched it up with a butterfly bandage.

"This should help it heal up nicely. I'd try to talk you into stopping by the ER for a few stitches, but I didn't want to push my luck."

"I appreciate the recommendation. This

should be good." He'd grown up working a cattle ranch, so it wasn't the first time he'd ended up with a scar on his body. Nor would it be the last. He thanked Samantha for doing a fine job, which she had.

She told him it was no trouble at all before closing up her bag and heading toward the driver's seat of her ambulance. He would've just patched himself up but didn't want to appear a hypocrite in front of Makena after urging her to seek care.

Before he could open his mouth to speak, Makena threw herself into his chest and buried her face. He stroked her long, silky hair, figuring this was a rare show of emotion for her.

He couldn't be certain how long they stood there. Being with her, it was like time had stopped, and nothing else mattered except making sure she was okay.

When she pulled back, his heart clenched as he looked at her. She wore the same expression as she had that last day of biology lab. He'd been so tempted to ask her out despite the fact that it had been made clear she was with someone else. It would've gone against everything he believed in. Honor. Decency. He'd never break the code of asking someone out who was married, in a relationship, or dating someone else.

He'd cleaned up his own relationship at home, realizing that he and Rebecca would never have the kind of spark that he'd felt with Makena. He'd decided right then and there, with his nineteen-year-old self, that he'd hold out for that feeling to come around again. Little did he know just how rare it could be.

All these years later, he'd never felt it again until recently. It was then he realized what he and Makena had had was special.

"It's not safe for me to be here anymore, Colton. I know you need a statement from me, but I'd like to keep my name as quiet as possible. He obviously found me here and he'll find me again. I'll be ready next time. I took his threats too lightly. Not anymore."

"I do need a statement from you. And I have no authority to force you to stay in Katy Gulch. Whether or not you do, a crime happened here in my jurisdiction. Someone's property was damaged and there was an attempted murder and that makes it my responsibility. So, whether you're here or not, I plan to investigate." Why did the news of her wanting to run away impale him?

She had every right to do what she felt was necessary to protect herself. Now that he knew her ex was in law enforcement, so many of her reactions made sense to him. That fact alone made a relationship between them practically impossible.

Given Colton's line of work, she would always be reminded of her ex.

Makena shook her head furiously. "I understand you have to file a report. Believe me when I say you don't want to chase this guy down. Look what he's capable of, Colton. You have a family. You have young boys who depend on you. I won't have your life taken away from them because of something I did."

"Is that what you believe? That any of this is somehow your fault?"

"I didn't mean it like that. I know what River did in the past and now is completely on him. I didn't deserve it then and I don't deserve it now. I won't take responsibility for any of his actions. That's all on him. But *I* brought that man to your doorstep. That's the responsibility I feel."

"You're right about one thing. You did nothing wrong."

Her chin quivered at hearing those

words, so he repeated them. "You did nothing wrong."

She was nodding her head and looked to be fighting back tears. "I know."

"Sometimes we just need to hear it from someone else."

"Thank you, Colton. You have no idea what you've done for me in the past twenty-four hours and how much that has truly meant to me, which is why I can't burden you any more than I have."

Colton had his hands up, stopping her from going down that road again. "In case you hadn't noticed, Makena, this is my job. This is what I do. And yes, there are personal risks. Believe me when I say that I don't take them lightly. Also, know that I take safety very personally. I have every intention of walking through the door every night to my boys as I watch them grow up. There is no other option in my mind. And if this had been any-one else but you in this situation, I would still be following the same protocol. Most law enforcement officials are there for all the right reasons. It's rare for them to go completely rogue or off the chain. But when they do, they aren't just a danger to one person. They will be a threat to women, to children and to men. That's not something I can live with on my conscience. Not to mention the fact that I'm a law enforcement officer. Being on this job is in my blood."

He stopped there. He'd said enough. He gave her a few moments to let that sink in while he walked her over to his SUV.

Makena took in a deep breath. "Okay." She blew the breath out.

Colton hoped that meant she'd heard what he said and was ready for him to continue his investigation.

"Let's do this. Let's make sure that River Myers never hurts another soul again. I'll tell you everything I know about him."

Colton helped her into the passenger seat before closing the door and claiming his spot. Pride filled his chest. It wasn't easy for anyone to go against someone they'd cared about or, worse yet, someone they were afraid of. It took incredible courage to do what she was doing, and he couldn't be prouder of her than he was right then.

After giving Colton a description of her ex, his badge number, his social security and his license plate, she dropped another bomb on him.

"Abuse is not the only thing he's guilty of. I don't know the names of the people he was talking to one night in my garage but I'd heard a noise and when I went to investigate, River flipped out. He rushed me back inside the house and threatened me. He told me that I had no idea what I'd just done. All I can figure is that I walked in on some kind of meeting between the three of them."

"Did you hear what they were talking about, by chance?"

"I wish I had. He rushed me out of there too early and I was too chicken to go back." Her hands were balled fists on her legs. "I guess they were planning something or talking about something they didn't want anyone else to know about. They sounded threatening and there was a handprint around River's throat. I thought I overheard something about getting someone to pay but I have no idea what that means."

"Were the other men in uniform?"

"No. They weren't. They were in regular street clothes but they acted like cops." That didn't mean they weren't officers.

"Did you get a good look at them?"

"Yes. As a matter of fact, I did. And I saw them here three days ago. It's the reason I ducked into the RV and didn't leave for three days straight."

That explained why she'd practically starved to death by the time she'd walked out to find food. So many things clicked in the back of his mind. Like the fact that she'd gone out in a driving rain when there were no cars out. It must have been to forage for food. The way she'd gobbled down that sandwich and apple made more sense to him now.

He'd wondered how long it had been since she'd had a meal.

"I knew I'd stuck around too long and I was preparing to move on. Seeing them scared me to the core. River had always been clear. If I left him, he would hunt me down and kill me. He would see the divorce as the ultimate betrayal."

Another thought dawned on Colton. River may not have been trying to kill her. His cohorts, on the other hand, seemed ready to do the job.

They could be in league with River. They may or may not be cops themselves, but they definitely could be doing his dirty work.

"Describe them to me in as much detail as you can remember."

Chapter Nine

"The first one I saw was around six feet tall. He had a football-player build, with a clean-shaven face. His hair was light red...kind of strawberry blond. He had a thick neck and big hands. Other than that, I remember that he had light skin and freckles." Makena remembered the men vividly because they were so different.

Colton nodded.

"The second guy had one of those 1970s mustaches on an otherwise clean face. Black hair with big bushy eyebrows. He had these puffed-out cheeks like he had a big wad of gum or tobacco in his jaws. His hair was short and thick and a little wavy. I remember that he was several inches shorter than Red. They were so distinct-looking and oddly matched. Opposites. That's what I remember about them from that night."

"Did you have a chance to hear their voices? Would you recognize them if you heard them?"

She shook her head.

"Cops?" he asked.

"I don't know for certain. I can't be one hundred percent sure. They looked like they were law enforcement. They had that cop carriage, if you know what I mean."

Colton nodded. He seemed to know exactly what she was talking about. There was just a cop swagger. Being on the job, wearing a holster for long shifts day in and day out caused them to hold their arms out a little more than usual. They also walked with the kind of confidence that said they could handle themselves in almost any situation. They had the training to back it up.

"What shift did your ex work?" Colton asked.

"Deep nights. He requested them. Said he liked to be out and about when everyone else was asleep." She couldn't imagine anything had changed in the past few months since she'd been gone, considering the fact that River had been on deep nights for almost fifteen years.

"A couple of my brothers work in law enforcement," he said.

"Oh yeah?"

"U.S. Marshals. They would help if we brought them up to speed." Colton had scribbled down descriptions of Red and Mustache Man. He also made notes about River's shift preference. Considering it was only ten thirty in the morning, River would be home and still asleep.

"I'm not sure it's such a good idea." A

lot was coming at her, fast. She needed a minute to process. "Can I think about it first?"

He nodded and then moved on. "Could he afford the residence you shared on his own?"

"I moved into his bachelor pad and fixed it up. It's likely that he's still there. He doesn't really like change."

Colton checked the clock on his dashboard. It was almost like he read her thoughts. He started the engine of his sport utility. "I have a few calls to make that might go a little easier in my office. You okay with that?"

What he was really asking was would she stay with him? She could read between the lines. Since she had nowhere to go, literally, and no friends in town, she nodded. The honest truth was that she didn't feel safe with anyone but Colton. Being with him was warmth and campfires despite the dangers all around.

She leaned her head back and brought her hands up to rub her temples. Her head hurt. A dull ache was forming between her eyes. The headache distracted her from her hip pain. Now, there was something. She was getting punchy.

Makena appreciated the fact that the ride to Colton's office was short. She climbed out of the sport utility, her hip reminding her that it wasn't quite finished with her yet.

The driver's-side door of a blue sports sedan popped open two spots down, the driver having cut off the engine almost the minute she stepped out of the SUV. Makena flinched.

The person held something toward Colton. As the youngish man, early thirties if she had to guess, bum-rushed them, Colton tensed. His gaze bounced from being locked onto the guy he seemed to recognize and then across the rest of the cars in the lot. The way he watched anything that moved reminded her just how out in the open they were in the parking lot.

The jerk with what she recognized as his phone in his hand caught up to them. "Sheriff O'Connor."

"Mike."

"Sir, do you care to comment on your sister's kidnapping and the recent crime wave in Katy Gulch?"

Colton stopped dead in his tracks. He turned to face the guy named Mike, who Makena assumed was a reporter. "That story has been dead for decades, Mike. What's wrong? Slow news week?"

"Sir, I—I—I…"

"I accept your apology, Mike. Now, if you don't mind, I have business to attend to in my office." Colton turned his back on the reporter and started walking toward the building. He said out the side of his mouth, "But if there are any new leads, you'll be the first to know."

Considering Colton's stiff demeanor, it was clear to Makena the story about his sister's kidnapping was off-limits.

Mike stood there, looking dumbfounded.

Makena heard what was said, and she couldn't help but think about the fact that Colton's father had just died. She wondered if the two incidents were connected in some way. That had to be unlikely, given that Colton himself had said his sister's kidnapping was decades old. Colton had also mentioned a kidnapping attempt on his newly minted sister-in-law's adopted daughter and then there was his father's death. A family like the O'Connors could be a target for any twisted individual who wanted to make a buck. A shudder raced through her. She could only imagine based on her experience of living in fear for the months on end what it must be like living on guard at all times.

Colton had mentioned that a couple of his brothers had gone on to become US marshals. He was sheriff. She had to wonder if their choices to go into law enforcement had anything to do with a need to protect each other and keep their family safe.

The minute Colton walked through the front door and into the lobby, a woman who seemed to be in her late sixties popped up from her desk, set the phone call she'd been on down, and ran over to give Colton a warm hug. The moment was sweet and the action seemed to come from a genuine place.

"Thank heavens you're okay." The woman had to be Gert, Makena guessed from the sound of her voice. It also made sense that she would be at Colton's office.

When Gert finally released him from the hug, he introduced her to Makena.

"I'm pleased as punch to meet you. I'm

sorry for the day you've had. Can I get you anything? Coffee? Water?"

"Coffee sounds great. Just point me in a direction and I can get my own cup." Makena echoed Gert's sentiments. Now that she'd had a minute to process the fact that her ex had tried to blow her to smithereens, she needed a strong cup of coffee.

"Don't be silly. I'd be happy to get you a cup. I just put on a fresh pot."

"If you're offering, I'll take a cup of that coffee, too." He placed his hand on the small of Makena's back and led her through a glass door that he had to scan his badge to enter. He hooked a right in what looked to be a U-shaped building and then led her halfway down the hall. His office was on the right.

"Make yourself comfortable," Colton said. "Is there anything else you'd like besides coffee?"

"No, thank you." The shock of the day's

events was starting to wear off. The annoying ringing noise was a constant companion as she moved to the leather sofa and then took a seat.

Colton moved behind his desk. "Professional courtesy dictates that I make a call to Mr. Myers's chief before questioning him."

"Won't that give River a heads-up that you want to speak to him?" The thought of being in the same room again with her ex fired more of that anger through her veins. It needed to be a courtroom, the next time. And he needed to be going to jail for a very long time. One way or another, she would find a way for justice to be served and keep him from harming other innocent people. But the River she knew wouldn't exactly lie down and take what was coming his way. Without a doubt, he'd deny any involvement.

The explosion and fire would have made certain there were no fingerprints.

When she really thought about the crime, it was an easy way on his part to get away with murder. No one would know her in Katy Gulch. That meant she would most likely have ended up a Jane Doe. She'd quit her job and disappeared. No one would miss her.

She could vanish and there was no one to notice. How sad had her life become since marrying him, since her mother's drawn-out illness, that Makena could die at the hands of her ex and no one would know?

The only person she knew in Katy Gulch was Colton. He would have had no reason to suspect a blast from the past. He wouldn't have been looking for her. And if she'd been badly burned, which seemed like the plan, her face would have been unrecognizable anyway. It had been a near-perfect setup.

She flexed and released her fingers a couple of times to work out some of the tension. She rolled her shoulders back and took in a couple of deep breaths. She couldn't imagine trying to hurt someone she supposedly cared about.

Colton's voice broke through her heavy thoughts. She realized he was on a call.

"Yes, sir. My name is Sheriff Colton O'Connor and I need to speak with Chief Shelton. This is a professional courtesy call and I need to speak to him about one of his officers." Colton was silent for a few beats. And then came, "Thank you, sir."

A few more beats of silence, and then someone must've picked up on the other line. Gert walked in about that same moment with two mugs of coffee in her hands. She set the first one down on Colton's desk, which was the closest to her. The other one she brought over to Makena, who accepted the offering and thanked Colton's secretary for her kindness.

Gert produced a couple packets of sugar and a pack of creamer from her pocket and set them down on the coffee table along with a stir stick. Gert made eye contact and nodded. The sincerity, warmth and compassion in her gaze settled over Makena. It was easy to see the woman had a heart of gold. She disappeared out of the room after Makena mouthed a thank-you.

"As I said before, this is a professional courtesy call to let you know that the name of one of your police officers came up in the course of an investigation today." Colton was silent for a moment. "Yes, sir. The officer's name is River Myers. A few more seconds of silence followed. "Is that right?" A longer pause. This time the silence dragged on. Colton glanced at her, caught her eye and then nodded. She could tell there was a storm brewing behind his cobalt eyes.

After Colton explained to the Dallas

police chief that he wanted to speak to River in connection with an attempted murder case, there was even more silence.

Colton ended the call by thanking the chief for his time and by promising that he would keep him abreast of his investigation.

"What did he say?" She waited for Colton to hang up before asking the question.

"He wished me luck with my investigation. He said his office was fully prepared to cooperate. And then he informed me that River Myers is on administrative leave pending an investigation."

Makena gasped as all kinds of horrible thoughts crossed her mind. "Did he say what River was being investigated for?"

Colton's earlier words that she needed to speak up so she could prevent anyone else from getting hurt slammed into her.

Had River done something to another woman he was in a relationship with?

"The chief said he really can't share a lot of details for an ongoing investigation, but in the spirit of reciprocity, he said an internal affairs division investigation was underway on two counts of police brutality and one count of extortion."

Relief washed over Makena that River wasn't already being looked at for murder. He was, now. "What does being placed on administrative leave mean?"

"It's basically where he would be required to hand in his department-issued weapons along with his badge until the investigation is over and it's decided whether or not any criminal charges would be filed." Colton took a sip of coffee.

Makena brought her hand up to her mouth. If River had still been on the job, they would know exactly where to find him. "Does this mean what I think? That he's out there somewhere? Going rogue?"

"That is a distinct possibility." Colton's grip on his coffee mug caused his knuckles to go white. With his free hand, he drummed his fingers on his desk. "I need to issue a BOLO with his name and description. I don't want my deputies being caught unawares if they happen to run into him personally or on a traffic stop."

Colton mentioned a couple of other things before jumping into action. Not five minutes later, he'd had Gert issue the BOLO, he'd started the report on the explosion, and he'd nearly polished off his second cup of coffee. Once he'd taken care of those preliminary details, he looked at her. "My next call needs to be to my mother. But first, I want to know where you stand. Will you stay with me until the investigation runs its course?"

The look on his face suggested he expected an argument. She had none.

"I appreciate the offer. You already know my concerns about bringing danger to your doorstep. And then there's your boys to consider."

"Don't worry about my sons. For the time being, they'll be safe at the ranch. I know my mom will pull through and yet she's the one I worry about the most. I have two new sisters-in-law I forgot about before, who I can ask to pitch in. The ranch has a lot of security in place already, and I don't mind adding to it. In fact, it might not be a bad idea for me to take you to my home there. Times will come up when I have to leave for the investigation or for work, and I want to know that you're safe."

Makena could stay on the ranch safely with all the extra security. She could not live with bringing danger around Colton and his children. "I'll stay with you at your apartment or I'll wait here at your office if you need to investigate someone without me there. But I won't go to the ranch. It's too dangerous for the people."

Colton rubbed the scruff on his chin. He took a sip of coffee. "That's fair."

She hoped so, because it was the only offer on the table. If she had to sit in the office for an entire day, she would. There was no way in hell she was going to risk his family. Granted, River wanted her. But she couldn't be certain that he wouldn't use one of them to draw her out. It was a gamble she had no intention of taking.

Makena rolled up her sleeves and drained her cup. She set the mug down on the coffee table. She placed her flat palms on her thighs and looked at Colton.

"What's next?"

"You tell me everything you can think of about your ex. His favorite restaurant. Whether or not he's a fisherman and has a fishing lease. Is he a hunter? Does he have a hunting license? Who are his friends? And then, I go track him down."

"Hold on there. I'm the best person to help find him. I want to go to Dallas with you."

"Not a chance. The agreement we just made was that you would stay here while I investigate. It's either here or my apartment. I need to know that I can trust you to do what you say you're going to do."

"I wouldn't lie to you. I just thought it would be easier to track him down with me involved."

"If you're his target and he sees you, it could be game over."

"I'm not arguing. However, trying to blow me to pieces on a timer once I thought I was safely inside an RV doesn't exactly make me feel like he wants to be connected to my murder in any way. In fact, he seems to be taking great pains to kill me without leaving any trail back to him."

"True enough. The explosion was most likely meant to cover his tracks. We also have to broaden the scope. You saw his friends…or…acquaintances might be a better word. You said yourself they were speaking in hushed tones. We can go after them, too. They might be acting on his behalf or they might be on their own."

"Oh, I doubt anyone would do that. Not with River's temper. He never struck me as the type to step aside."

"We have to keep unbiased eyes on the case and we have to follow the evidence. Right now, you saw two people from your past in town three days ago and that spawned you to disappear into the RV."

"Allegedly saw. I mean, they were far away and I can't be one hundred percent certain it was them."

"Okay. What are the chances the two guys you saw, even at a distance, weren't the men you saw in your garage?" He was playing devil's advocate. She could see that. Looking at the case from every angle probably made him a good investigator.

It was impossible for Makena not to lead with emotions in this case. For one, the explosion was targeted at her. And for another, River's threats echoed in her mind. To her thinking, he was delivering on threats he'd made six months ago.

Chapter Ten

Colton spent the next hour getting to know River Myers. He then made a quick call to his mother, and she agreed the twins staying on with her would be for the best, at least for a couple of days.

He knew better than anyone that investigations often took far longer than that, but he hoped for a break in this one. If Makena's ex was determined to erase her and she was constantly at Colton's side, he would have to get through Colton first. Makena had made a list of River's known hangouts. Colton had handed the list over to Gert, who'd meticulously called each one to ask when the last time River had been in.

So far, no one had seen or heard from River for the past month. Of course, the couple of places that were known cop hangouts most likely wouldn't admit to seeing him if he was standing in front of their faces.

Other than that, he frequented a popular Tex-Mex restaurant and a couple of taco chains. None of the managers or employees admitted to seeing the man in the past few weeks if not a month.

The timing of River sticking to himself coincided with when he was put on leave according to the chief. It was odd, since the guy would've had more free time on his hands. Usually, that meant being seen in his favorite haunts more often. In River's case, he seemed to be hunkering down.

A call to one of his neighbors revealed that it didn't seem like he'd been home, either. There were no lights left on in the evenings, and the neighbor hadn't seen his truck in a couple of weeks.

"What are the chances he has a new girlfriend?" Colton asked Makena.

She looked up from her notebook, where she'd been trying to recall and write down all the places he could've possibly gone to.

"Anything is possible. Right?" She tapped her pencil on the pad. "I mean, he's not really the type to be alone and he was served with divorce papers not long after I disappeared. I worked through my lawyer to finish up the paperwork."

"If River is spending all his time at a new girlfriend's house, it might be harder to track him down." His personal phone number had changed. Colton had his guess as to why that might have happened.

As word spread about the morning's incident, Colton's phone started ringing off the hook. Everyone in the community wanted to pitch in and help find the person responsible for blowing up Mrs. Dillon's RV. Colton couldn't give any more details than that and it was impossible to keep this story completely quiet considering how much neighbors watched out for each other in Katy Gulch.

After hours of receiving and making phone calls, Colton realized it was past dinnertime. Not a minute later, Gert knocked on the office door. It was a courtesy knock because Colton had a long-standing open-door policy.

"It might be time to take a break," Gert said. They both knew she would go home and continue working on the case, but it was her signal she was heading out.

"Let me know if you get any leads or figure out anything that I've missed," Colton said. He stretched out his arms and yawned, realizing he'd been sitting in the same position for hours. It was no wonder his back was stiff. His ears were still ringing from the explosion this morning but there was improvement there, too.

"You know I will, sir." Gert waved to Makena before exiting the room. Before she got more than a few steps down the hall she shouted back at them. "I'll lock the front door."

Colton turned to Makena. "What do you think about taking this back to my apartment? We should probably get up and get our blood moving. And then there's dinner. You must be starved by now."

"That's probably a good idea. I'm not starving, but I could eat. The bags of nuts and trail mix that Gert has been bringing me have tided me over."

"I'll just close up a couple of files and log out and then we can go." Colton tried not to notice when Makena stood up and stretched just how long her legs were. She had just the right amount of soft curves, and all he could think about was running his hand along those gorgeous lines...

He forced his gaze away from her hips—a place he had no business thinking about. He straightened up his desk and then closed out of the files on his desktop. His laptop had access to the same system, and he could get just as much done at home. He figured Makena would be more comfortable there anyway.

It also occurred to him that she'd lost everything she owned except the clothes on her back. He stood up and pushed his chair in. He gripped the back of his chair with both hands. "We can stop off anywhere you need on the way to my house. I'm sure you want a change of clothes and something to sleep in."

"I appreciate the offer, but pretty much everything I own was blown up. I don't have any ID or credit cards with me." He realized that she wouldn't want to carry ID in case she got picked up. Now that he knew her ex was a cop, he understood why she'd gone to the lengths she had to keep her identity a secret.

"How about I take care of it for you? It really wouldn't be any trouble—"

"You're already doing so much for me, Colton. It's too much to ask. I'll be fine with what I have."

"I promise it isn't. We don't have to do anything fancy. We can stop off at one of those big-box stores. There's one on the way home. We can let you pick up a few supplies. It would be a loan. Just until you get back on your feet. I have a feeling once we lock this jerk away for good, you'll get back on your feet in no time. For old times' sake, I'd like to be the one to give you a temporary hand up."

Colton hoped he'd put that in a way that didn't offend her. He wasn't trying to give her a handout. All he wanted was to give her a few comfort supplies while they located the bastard who'd tried to kill her.

She raked her top teeth over her bottom lip, a sure sign she was considering his offer. Then again, with her back against the wall, she might not feel like she had any options.

"I promise it's no trouble, and if you don't want to take the stuff with you, you could always leave it at my place. One of my new sisters-in-law will probably fit the same clothes. Renee looks to be about your size, if leaving them would make you feel better. It would certainly make me feel better to be able to help you out. Besides, you're probably the only reason I passed biology lab."

That really made her laugh. "I was terrible at biology lab. If you hadn't helped me, I would've failed and I'm pretty certain I dragged your grade down."

"I might have been better at the actual

work than you were, but you were the only reason I kept going to class."

Her smile practically lit up the room. It was nice to make her smile for a change after all she'd been through. She deserved so much better.

"I tell you what. I'll let you buy me some new clothes. But once this is over, maybe I can stick around a few days and watch the boys for you as a way to pay you back. I'm not sure I'm any good with kids that age and they might not even like me, but I'm willing to try. And who knows, we might actually have some fun. It would make me feel so much better if I can do something nice for you."

"Deal." He wouldn't look a gift horse in the mouth. This was something nice, and she made a good point. He was halting his nanny search so he could throw himself completely into this investigation. As much as the process would take time, he was also keenly aware that the colder the trail, the colder the leads. His best bet at nailing the bastard would come in a window of opportunity he had in the next seventy-two hours. If the investigation dragged on longer than that, the apprehension rate would drop drastically.

Unless there was another attempt. Colton didn't even want to consider that option.

"Do you want to take a minute to order a few things on the laptop? We can put a rush on the order, and they'll have it ready by the time we swing through. I just need to turn off a few lights and double-check the break room." He handed his laptop over.

"Sure." She sat down in one of the leather club chairs across from his desk and studied the screen as he headed down the hallway.

Turning off the lights had been an excuse to give her a few minutes alone to order. In reality, he didn't like the idea of her going out in public where she'd be exposed. A skilled rifleman could take her out from the top of a building or beside a vehicle.

And then there was the gossip mill to consider. Most of the time, he didn't mind it. For the most part, people were trying to be helpful by sharing information. Being seen with him would be news. Like it or not, the O'Connors were in the public eye and people seemed to enjoy discussing the details of his family's private lives.

He took his time checking rooms before returning. The laptop was closed. She stood up the minute she heard him come in the room. "Ready?"

"All set," she said, handing over the device. He tucked it under one arm before placing his hand on the small of her back and leading her out the rear of the building. He guided her down the hall and outside, deciding it would be safer to take his personal vehicle home.

His pickup truck was parked out back.

"I don't want to run into Mike or anyone else sniffing around for a story." It was true. But he also didn't want to risk going out the same way he'd come in, just in case River or one of his cohorts was watching. That part Colton decided to keep to himself.

Colton finally exhaled the breath he'd been holding when they were safely inside his truck and on the road. It was past seven o'clock, and it wouldn't be dark for another hour and a half this time of year.

Being out in the daylight made him feel exposed. He kept his guard up, searching the face of every driver as he passed them. He stopped off at the box store and pulled into the pickup lane. A quick text later, an employee came running out to the designated curbside area.

Colton thanked the guy and handed him

a five-dollar bill. The rest of the ride to his apartment took all of ten minutes. He pulled up to the garage and punched in the security code before zipping through the opened gate.

From a security standpoint, the place wouldn't be that difficult to breech on foot. But the gate kept other drivers from coming in and closed quickly enough after he pulled through that it would be impossible to backdraft him.

Colton had spent part of the drive thinking through something that had been bugging him since he'd gotten off the phone with the DPD chief. If River was being investigated for serious charges like police brutality and extortion, there had to be a reasonable complainant involved. Considering there were several charges against him, he wondered what kind of huddle Makena could've walked into that night, when she'd interrupted River and the other two men.

It was obviously a meeting of some kind. The fact that River had ushered her away so fast meant that he was trying to protect his group, or her. Possibly both. In his twisted mind, he probably believed that he loved his wife.

Abusers usually thought they cared for their partners. Forget that their version of caring was tied up with control and abuse, sometimes physical. When they realized that, they seemed to have some sense of remorse. For others, it was just a way of life.

Thinking back, Colton wondered if Makena's life would've turned out differently if he'd somehow plucked up the courage to ask her out.

But then, his own life might've turned out differently, too. Having the twins was one of the best things that had ever happened to him. He wouldn't trade his boys for the world. And even though his wife had died, he wouldn't trade the years of friendship they'd had, either.

Since regret was about as productive as stalking an ant to find cheese, he didn't go there often. Life happened. He'd lost Rebecca. He'd gained two boys out of their relationship.

Makena's life might not have turned out differently even if they had dated. There was no way to go back and find out. And even if they could…change one thing and the ripple effect could be far-reaching.

Returning his focus to the case, he thought about Red and Mustache Man. The what-if questions started popping into his mind.

What if Red and Mustache had been working to shake someone down? Considering one of the charges against River was extortion, it was a definite possibility.

If Mustache and Red had come to Katy

Gulch, were they sticking around? Were they acting alone? Were they after her because they thought she'd heard something in her garage that night?

Alarm bells sounded at the thought. He felt like he was onto something there.

This could've been an attempt to... what?

Hold on. Colton had it. If River had gone into hiding and the guys blew up Makena, would that be enough to bring him out?

COLTON THREW A PIZZA in the oven while Makena mixed together a salad from contents she'd found in the fridge. Working in the kitchen with her was a nice change to a frozen dinner in front of his laptop after the boys were in bed.

They'd just sat down at the island to eat when his cell phone buzzed. He glanced at the screen and saw Gert's name. Makena was sitting next to him, so he tilted the screen in her direction before taking the call. He held the phone to his ear.

"This is Colton. I'm going to put you on speaker. Is that okay?" There was some information that was sensitive enough that Makena shouldn't hear.

"Fine by me, sir."

Colton put the call on speaker and set it in between him and Makena on the island. "Okay. Makena and I are listening."

"Sir, Deputy Fletcher was canvassing in Birchwood and stopped off at a motel along the highway. He got a hit." Her voice practically vibrated with excitement. Gert loved the investigation process. "The clerk told Deputy Fletcher a man matching River Myers's description had been staying at her motel for the past four days. The clerk's name is Gloria Beecham and this place is a rent-by-the-hour type, if you know what I mean. She said he was a cash customer. Given the amount of time he'd been there and the fact that he kept the Do Not Disturb sign on the door the whole time, housekeeping was freaked out by the guy."

Colton wasn't surprised. Hotels and motels had tightened up their processes to ensure every room was checked.

"Housekeeping alerted the clerk to the fact. She made a call to let him know that housekeeping had to check his room every twenty-four hours by law. She said that when they came to clean, he would stand in the corner of the room with the door open and his arms crossed over his chest."

"Odd behavior," Colton noted.

"It sure is." She made a tsk noise. "They never did find anything suspicious, and honestly, admitted to getting in and out of there just as fast as they could."

"And this mystery man matched River's description?" he asked.

"Yes, sir."

"He was staying in the room alone?" This could be a solid lead. Colton looked at Makena, who was on the edge of her seat.

"Yes, sir."

"Did they say whether anyone else ever came in or out of the room?"

"No. No one to her knowledge. She started keeping an eye on the room by the camera mounted outside. This place has no interior spaces. It's the kind of place where you park right in front of your door and use a key to go straight inside. So there are cameras along the exterior overhangs. She said it was something the owner had insisted on installing over a year ago. The funny thing is, he struck her as odd because his face was always pointed the opposite direction of the nearest camera."

"He was smart enough to realize that cameras might be in use."

"So much so, in fact, he wore a ball cap

most of the time. He kept his chin tucked to his chest as he walked in and out of the building."

"Did they, by chance, get a make and model on his vehicle?" Colton asked.

"No, sir. They did not. He never parked close enough to the door for the cameras to pick up his vehicle."

Colton wished there were parking lot cameras. Even a grainy picture would give him some idea of the kind of vehicle River was driving, if that was in fact him. The coincidence was almost too uncanny.

The possibility the clerk could've picked up on any details of the bombing case from the media was nil. He'd kept a very tight rein on the details of the morning's event on purpose. He'd released a statement that said there had been an incident involving an RV and a homemade explosive device, and there'd been no casualties or injuries. Technically, that part was true. The scratch on his arm would be fine and his hearing would return to normal in a few days. The ringing was already easing.

Evidence was mounting against River.

"And this witness was certain, without a shadow of a doubt, that the man at the motel matched the BOLO?"

"Not one hundred percent," Gert admitted. "She said she wouldn't exactly bet her life on it, but it was probably him."

Colton cursed under his breath. He needed a witness who would testify they were certain it was River, not someone who *thought* it might be him.

"This is something. At least we have someone who can most likely place him in town or at least near town. Birchwood is a half-hour drive from here."

"That's right, sir."

"Is he still there, by chance?" He probably should've asked this already, except that Gert would've known to lead with it.

"That's a negative sir." Gert's frustration came through the line in her sigh. "You're going to love this one. He checked out first thing this morning, at around six thirty."

Colton had figured as much, even though he'd hoped for a miracle. River, or anyone in law enforcement, would be smart enough to stay on the move. "You mentioned the place was basically a cash-and-carry operation. Is that right?"

"Yes, sir. And I confirmed that the person who'd stayed in room 11 paid with cash."

"Good work, Gert." Colton pressed his lips together to keep from swearing.

Makena issued a sharp sigh. "So close."

"Thanks for the information, Gert. It gives us confirmation that we're on the right track."

"My pleasure, sir. And you know me. Once I'm on a trail, I stick with it."

"I've never been sure who was the better investigator between the two of us. I appreciate all your efforts." He knew it made Gert's chest swell with pride to hear those words. He meant them, too. She was a formidable investigator and she'd proven to be invaluable in many cases.

Colton thanked her again before ending the call.

"I knew it was only a matter of time before he caught up to me." Makena's voice was a study in calm as she stabbed her fork into her salad. Almost too calm. And yet, Colton figured she was much like the surface of the river. Calm on top with a storm raging below the surface.

If River checked out at six o'clock this morning, he could've set the bomb at the RV. He'd had a specific detonation in mind. It made sense to Colton that he'd wanted Makena to be stepping on the platform as she headed inside the RV to blow her up. Otherwise, if she stepped on the platform to go outside, then the bomb could've been a warning. It was possible, maybe unlikely, the ordeal was meant to be a scare tactic.

Without knowing much about River, it was difficult to ascertain which. But what would he have to gain by scaring her months later?

River had had some time on his hands recently to stew on his situation. It was clear the guy had a temper. He'd used that on Makena during their marriage. And yet a hothead didn't tend to be as calculating. That type was usually more spontaneous.

In Colton's years of investigating domestic violence cases, of which there'd been sadly too many, it was generally a crime of passion that led to murder. A spouse walked in on another spouse having an affair. The unsuspecting spouse got caught up in the moment, grabbed a weapon and committed murder.

Makena had not had an affair in this case. She'd left. That was a betrayal someone like River wouldn't take lightly.

Chapter Eleven

Makena pushed around a piece of lettuce on her plate. The fact that River had been in town at the very least on the morning someone had attempted to take her life sat heavy on her chest. It wouldn't do any good to look back and question how on earth she'd ever trusted him in the first place.

It was time to move forward. And then something dawned on her. "Did I hear right? Did Gert say River checked into that hotel four nights ago?"

"That's the same thing I heard. Gert will write it all up in a report, but yeah, that's what I heard." Colton rocked his head. He pushed the phone away from their plates.

"So River shows up four days ago. It's now been four days since I saw Red and Mustache Man." A picture was taking shape, but it was still too fuzzy to make out all the details.

"So these three have met in your garage and now they are in town at the same time without staying in the same room. We don't know if they rented a room next door." Colton got up, found a notepad and pen and then reclaimed his seat. He scratched out a note for them to check with the early-morning-shift clerk to see if anyone matching the description of Red or Mustache had checked in or been seen coming into or out of River's room.

"Gert said River had no visitors," she corrected, distinctly remembering Gert's words.

"True." He scratched out the last part.

"Which didn't mean they didn't meet up somewhere."

She was already thinking the same thing.

"Maybe they thought I overhead them and that's why I left my husband. Maybe in their twisted-up minds they think I know something, which meant the meeting in the garage could've been some kind of planning meeting."

Colton was already nodding his head. "It makes sense. When we look at murder or an attempted murder case, we're always looking for the motive. In your case, one could make the argument that River was still jealous months after you left and that it took him that long to hunt you down. That would make sense. It's a story that, unfortunately, has been told before. The twist in this case is Mustache and Red. If River was here because of a jealousy that he couldn't let go of or because he didn't want you to ever be with anyone else, which is another motive in domestic cases, there wouldn't have been anyone else with him."

"That's exactly my thinking. So if I did walk in on a meeting that day and they think I know something, which I assure you I don't no matter how much I wish I did, they're willing to kill me to make sure I'm silenced. River has already gotten in trouble with his department for extortion. At least, he's under investigation for it." They were finally on a path that made some sense to her. Granted, it was still twisted and unfair, and she didn't like anything about it, period, but it made sense. "Okay, what do we do next?"

"Tonight? We eat. We try to set the case aside at least for a little while. Overly focusing on something and overthinking it only creates more questions. Tomorrow, six a.m., we pay a visit to Gloria Beecham and see if she remembers seeing Red or Mustache anywhere in the area.

If we can link those three up, it's a story that makes sense."

Colton was holding something back.

"What is it?"

"There's another story that says all three of them are in town and in a race to see who gets to you first."

Makena shuddered at the thought. It was a theory that couldn't be ignored. It would still take a while to wrap her thoughts around the fact that anyone would want her dead, let alone three people. But it was possible each person was acting on his own, trying to be the one to get to her first to see what she knew and if she had evidence against any one of them.

"Think you can eat something?" Colton motioned toward her plate. "It's important to keep up your strength."

"I can try." She surprised herself by finishing the plate a few minutes later. Colton was right about one thing—overthinking the case would most likely drive her insane.

When the plates were empty, she picked up hers and headed toward the sink. She stopped midway. "I can clean yours while I'm up." At least the ringing noise in her ears was substantially better if not her left hip. The bruise was screaming at her, making its presence known. Colton was right. All she wanted was to stand under a warm shower and to curl up on the couch and watch TV to take her mind off the situation.

Colton was on his feet in the next second, plate in hand. He was such a contrast to River, who, in all the years she spent with him, basically set a plate down wherever he was and got up and walked away without a thought about how it got cleaned and ended up back in the cabinet the next day. He'd blamed his disinclination to do the house chores on being tired after working the deep night shift. The truth was that he thrived on that schedule. And the other truth was that he was lazy.

"It's not that hard for me to rinse off a second dish and put it in the dishwasher."

Colton set his dish down next to the sink. "For the last year, I've done everything for myself. Well, for myself and two little ones. I'm not trying to be annoying by doing everything myself, but I can see how that might get on someone's nerves. Especially someone who is strong and independent, and also used to doing things for herself. The truth is, being in the kitchen together making dinner tonight, even though it was literally nothing but pizza and salad, was probably my favorite time in this kitchen since I moved in."

Well, damn. Colton sure had a way with words. His had just touched her heart in the best possible way and sent warmth rocketing through her. She stopped what she was doing, turned off the spigot and leaned into him.

"It's been a pretty crazy twenty-four hours since we literally ran into each other, but it's really good to see you again, Colton."

It was so easy in that moment to turn slightly until her body was flush with his and tilt her face toward him. She pushed up on her tiptoes and pressed a kiss to his soft, thick lips. Being around Colton again was the easiest thing despite the electricity constantly pinging between them. Instead of fighting it…she was so very tired of fighting…she leaned into it.

Colton took a deep breath. And then he brought his hands up to cup her face. He ran his thumb along her jawline and then her chin as he trailed his lips in a line down her neck. He feathered a trail of hot kisses down her neck and across her shoulder. She placed the flat of her palms against his solid-walled chest, letting her fingers roam.

She smoothed her hands toward his shoulders and then up his neck, letting her fingers get lost in that thick mane of his as he deepened the kiss.

There was so much fire and energy and passion in the kiss. Her breath quickened and her pulse raced. Kissing Colton was better than she'd imagined it could be. No man had ever kissed her so thoroughly or made her need from a place so deep inside her.

He splayed one of his hands across the small of her back and pressed her body against his. Then his hands dropped, and she lifted her legs up and with help wrapped them around his midsection. He dropped his head to the crook of her neck.

Colton held onto her for a long minute in that position before he released a slow, guttural groan and found her lips again.

He fit perfectly and all she wanted to do was get lost with him.

THE ATTRACTION THAT had been simmering between Colton and Makena ignited into a full-blown blaze. He wanted nothing more than to strip down and bury himself deep inside her.

Her fingernails dug into the flesh of his shoulders. Considering her injury, this was about as far as he could let things go between them. There was another reason. A more obvious one. He knew without a doubt that taking their relationship to the next level would be a game changer for him, and he hoped it would be for her, too.

But she had trust issues and he still hadn't gotten over the loss of his best friend. Besides, as much as Makena fit him in every possible way, he had zero time to commit to a new relationship. He had the boys to think about and the fact that they might not be comfortable with him moving a stranger into the house. Somewhere in the back of his mind, his brain tried to convince him these were excuses. Maybe they were.

But if he was ready, he doubted his mind would try to come up with reasons they shouldn't be together. The biggest of which was the fact that she hadn't gotten over the experience with her ex.

Colton had seen that fear in her eyes one too many times. Granted, her anxiety had never been aimed at him and he would never do anything knowingly to hurt her. He wouldn't have to. His badge and gun might prove to be a problem for her.

Plus, she'd changed her life in every sense of the word. She needed to re-emerge and find a footing in her new life.

Makena moaned against his lips, and it was about the sexiest damn thing he'd ever heard. Let this go on too much longer and no cold shower in the world would be able to tame the blaze. Because he was just getting started.

He dropped his hands from her face, running his finger down to the base of her neck. He lowered his hand to her full breast and then ran his thumb along her nipple. It beaded under his touch and sent rockets of awareness through his body. Every single one of his muscles cried out for the sweet release only she could give. His need for Makena caused a physical ache.

Sleeping together at this point would only complicate the relationship. She was beginning to open up to him more and more. He sensed she was beginning to lean on him, and he liked the fact her trust in him was growing.

She needed to be sure how he felt about her before taking this to the next level. And since he was just now trying to figure that out himself, he pulled back and touched his forehead to hers. Their breathing was raspy. A smile formed on his lips.

Having twin sons had sure made one helluva grown-up out of him. Not that he'd taken sex lightly in the past. He preferred serial dating before he married Rebecca, and always made certain that his partners knew one hundred percent that the relationship would be based on mutual physical attraction. The likelihood anything emotional or permanent would come out of it was off the table.

"What is it, Colton? What's wrong? Did I do something?"

"You? Not a chance. It's me. And before you think I'm giving you the whole 'it's not you, it's me' speech, it really is me. I think whatever we have brewing between us could turn out to be something special. But the timing is off. I think we both realize that." He almost couldn't believe those words had just come out of his mouth. They were true. They needed to be said. But, damn.

He felt the need to explain further, because he didn't want her to be embarrassed or have any regrets. "For the record, I think that was probably up there with the best kisses of my life."

He could feel her smiling.

"Okay, I lied. That was the best kiss of my life. And it gets me in trouble because I don't want to stop there. I want more. And when I say more, I don't just mean physical." He could almost hear the wheels spinning in her brain and could sense she was about to do some major backpedaling.

"I hear what you're saying, Colton. I feel whatever this is happening between us, too. I don't exactly have anything to give right now." Ouch. Those words hurt more than he was expecting them to.

"You don't have to explain any of that to me. I feel the same."

"I'm sorry. This is the second time I've put you in this position. I promise not to do it again." She pulled back and put her hands up in the surrender position, palms out.

"Well, that's disappointing to hear." Colton laughed, a rumble from deep in his chest rolling up and out.

She looked at him with those clear blue eyes, so honest and still glittering with desire. The way his heart reacted, he thought he might've made a huge mistake in pulling back. Logic said that he had done the right thing in preparing her. His life didn't have room for anyone else, and she was just about to figure out what her new life was going to be. She didn't need him inserting himself right in the middle and possibly confusing her.

A sneaky little voice in the back of his mind said his defense mechanisms were kicking into high gear. He hushed that because it was time to think about something else.

"We could watch a movie to take our minds off things. We could talk." Normally, that last option would've felt like pulling teeth with no Novocain. But he actually liked talking to Makena. Go figure.

"I think what I would like more than anything is to curl up on the sofa with you and turn the fireplace on low. And maybe have something warm to drink. Maybe something without caffeine."

"Sounds like a plan. As far as the hot beverage without caffeine, I'm kind of at a loss on that one."

It was her turn to laugh. She reached up and grabbed a fistful of his shirt and tugged him toward her. She stopped him just before their lips met. "Thank you, Colton. You've brought alive parts of me that I honestly didn't know existed anymore. You've shown me what a strong, independent man can be."

This time she didn't push forward and press a kiss to his lips, and disappointment nearly swallowed him.

He smiled at her compliment and squeezed her hand, needing to refocus before he headed down that emotional path again.

"Good luck if you want something warm in this house that doesn't have caffeine."

"If you have water, a stove and maybe a lemon or honey, I can get by just fine."

"I definitely have honey. It's in the cupboard. Gert makes a point of bringing some back for everyone in the office when she visits honeybee farms. She's made a goal to visit every one in the state before the end of the year. I should have a few bottles in there to choose from. As far as lemons go, I actually might have a few of those in the bin inside the fridge.

I'll just make a call and check on my boys. I really want to hear their voices before they go to sleep. So if you'll excuse me, I'll take the call in the other room while you make up your warm batch of honey-lemon water."

His smile was genuine, and when she beamed back at him his heart squeezed. His traitorous heart would have to get on board with the whole "he needed to slow the train down" plan. It was on a track of its own, running full steam ahead.

Makena pushed him back a little bit in a playful motion. He hesitated for just a second, holding her gaze just a little too long, and his heart detonated when he turned to walk away. He exhaled a sigh and grabbed his phone off the granite island before heading into the bedroom.

He gave himself a few moments to shake off the haze in his mind from kissing Makena. He was still in a little bit of shock that one kiss could ignite that level of passion in him. He chalked it up to going too long without sex. That had to be the reason. He hadn't felt a flame burning like that in far too long.

After a few more deep breaths, he was at a ready point to hear his sons' little babbling voices. He pulled up his mother's contact and let his thumb hover over her number.

He dropped his thumb onto the screen and put the phone to his ear. It took a couple of rings for his mother to pick up. When she did, he could hear the sounds of his little angels in the background, laughing. He'd recognize those voices anywhere.

"Hi, son. I was just drying off the boys after their baths. How are you doing?" she asked. He listened for any signs of distress in her voice that meant taking care of the boys was too much for her right now.

"All is well here. We're moving forward with the investigation and I'll be up and out early tomorrow morning to go interview a potential witness. Making progress." Hearing his sons' laughter in the background warmed his heart.

"Colton, what's really wrong?" His mom could read him and his brothers better than a psychic.

"The case. I know the intended target from college. We go way back and she's a good person. She definitely doesn't deserve what's being handed to her." It would do no good to lie to his mother. She'd be able to hear it in his tone and he wouldn't feel good about it anyway. He'd been honest with her since seventh grade, after he'd hidden his phone in his room so he could call Rebecca when they were supposed to be asleep.

A young Colton hadn't slept a wink that night. He'd come clean about the deception in the morning and his mother said he'd punished himself enough. She expected him to leave his phone downstairs before he went up to bed just like the others did. Garrett had always sneaked back down to get his, but that was Garrett and beside the point.

Lying had taught Colton that he was an honest person.

Plus, his mother had been around him and his brothers who worked in law enforcement long enough to realize they wouldn't be allowed to divulge details about an ongoing investigation. She wouldn't dig around.

And she wouldn't ask. There were lines families in law enforcement never crossed.

"I'm sorry to hear such a nice-sounding person is having a rough go of it." He could hear more of that innocent laughter come across the line and he figured his mother knew exactly the distraction he needed. "The boys have had a wonderful day. They've been angels with just enough spunk in them for me to know they're O'Connor boys through and through."

"That's good to hear."

"Do you want me to put them on the line? I can put the phone in between them. They're here on the bed. Well, mostly here on the bed. Renee is here helping me and they keep trying to move to get away from the lotion." His mom laughed. It sounded genuine, and there'd been too much of that missing in her life over the past few months. It made him feel a lot less guilty about having the boys stay over with her for a few days. They might be just the distraction she needed.

"I would love it. Put them on." He could hear shuffling noises, which he assumed was her putting the phone down.

Her mouth was away from the receiver when she said, "Hey, boys. Guess who is calling you? It's your Dada."

It warmed his heart the way his family had accepted Silas and Sebastian despite the circumstances of their birth.

"Hey, buddies. I hope you are behaving for your Mimi and Aunt Renee." In truth, there wasn't a whole lot to say to one-year-olds. All he really wanted to hear was the sound of their giggles. Knowing how well they were being cared for and how much his mother loved them. It was kind of Renee to help.

One of the twins shrieked, "Dada!"

The other one got excited and started chanting the same word. Colton didn't care how or why his boys had come into his life. He was a better man for having them. He kept the phone to his ear and just listened.

A few minutes later, his mother came back on the line.

"Well, these two are ready for a little snack before bedtime," she said.

"Sounds good, Mom." He wanted to

ask how she was really doing but figured this wasn't the time. Instead, he settled on, "They really love you."

"Well, that's a good thing because I love them more. And I love you." There was a genuine happiness to her tone that made Colton feel good.

They said their goodbyes and ended the call. Colton glanced at the clock. It was after eight. He needed to grab a shower and get some shut eye soon. Four o'clock in the morning would come early and he wanted to be at the motel the minute the clerk started work.

Colton took a quick shower, toweled off and then threw on some sweatpants and a T-shirt. By the time he joined Makena in the other room, she was curled up on the couch. She'd figured out how to flip the switch to turn on the fireplace. He didn't want to dwell on how right it felt to see her sitting there in his home, on his sofa, looking comfortable and relaxed.

If it was just the two of them and she was in a different mental space, letting this relationship play out would be a no-brainer. But he had his children to think about and how the loss of their mother at such a young age would affect their lives. He also had to consider how bringing someone into their lives who could leave again might impact them. He couldn't see himself getting into a temporary relationship or introducing them to someone who might not stick around for the long haul.

"Shower's free. I left a fresh towel out for you and a washcloth. It's folded on the sink," he said, trying to ignore his body's reaction to her. His heart—traitor that it was—started beating faster against his rib cage.

Sitting there, smiling up at him, Makena was pure temptation. A temptation he had to ignore—for his own sanity.

Chapter Twelve

The shower was amazing and quick. Makena couldn't help but think about the case, despite trying to force it from her thoughts. It was impossible for questions not to pop into her mind after the update they'd received from Gert.

It was probably odd to appreciate the fact that she knew River. He had a physical description and a job. She couldn't imagine being targeted by someone without any idea who it could be or why.

Granted, in her case, the why was still a question mark. It could be his jealous nature. Or it could be that he believed she'd overheard something.

At least she wouldn't walk down the street next to the person targeting her without realizing it. Even Red and Mustache were on her radar.

And then there was Colton. She couldn't imagine having a better investigator or a better human being on her side. He'd grown into quite an incredible person, not that she was surprised. His cobalt blue eyes had always been just a little too serious and a little too intense even in college. He saw things most people would never notice. After hearing more about his family, she was starting to get a better understanding of him and what made him tick.

To say her feelings for him were complicated barely scratched the surface. She got dressed and brushed her teeth before venturing into the living room.

Colton sat in front of the fire, studying his laptop. Her heart free-fell at the sight of him looking relaxed and at ease. Butterflies flew in her stomach and she was suddenly transported back to biology lab at the time they had first met. Those feelings were very much alive today and sent rockets of need firing through her.

"Hey, I thought we agreed. No more working on the case tonight." She moved to the kitchen and heated more water. The lemon and honey water had done the trick earlier.

"I was just mapping out our route to the motel tomorrow morning. I wanted to be ready to go so that we're there the moment Gloria Beecham checks in for work."

"That sounds like a plan." The buzzer on the microwave dinged and she poured the warm water into the mug she'd used earlier.

"It's about a half hour's drive, so we should probably get on the road at five thirty at the latest."

"In the morning?" She gripped the mug

and added a slice of lemon along with another teaspoon of honey. After stirring the mixture, she made her way back to the sofa, noticing how badly her attempt at humor had missed the mark.

Colton continued to study the screen without looking up. She hoped she hadn't offended him earlier before the showers but the air in the room had definitely shifted. A wall had come up.

Makena pulled her legs up and tucked her feet underneath her bottom. She sat a couple of feet from Colton and angled herself toward him. From this distance, she'd be less likely to reach out and touch him. The feel of his silk-over-steel muscles was too much temptation. It would be so easy to get lost with him.

But then what?

There was no way she wanted to do anything that might drive a wedge between her and Colton. He was her best and only friend right then. She had no plans to cut off her lifeline. An annoying voice in the back of her head called her out on the excuses.

"So, the way I understand it, there's a story behind why everyone in law enforcement got there. What's yours?" She wanted to know why he'd chosen this profession versus taking up ranching.

He chuckled, a low rumble in his chest. "Do you mean more than the fact that I grew up with five brothers, all of whom were close in age?"

"That would challenge anyone's sense of justice," she laughed.

"I think it was always just inside me." He closed the laptop and shifted it off his lap and onto the sofa. Then he turned to face her. "We all used to play Cops and Robbers. Growing up on a ranch, we had plenty of room to roam and enough time to use our imagination. I was always drawn to the cop. For a while, I tried to tell myself that I was a rancher.

Don't get me wrong, ranching is in my blood and it's something I think I've always known I'd do at some point. We all pitch in, especially me before the boys came. I think I always knew it was just a matter of time. I want to take my place at the ranch. Later. I'm just not ready. So in college, when my parents tried to get me to go to the best agricultural school in the state, I rebelled. Our university had a pretty decent business school, and that's how I convinced my parents it was right for me. They weren't really trying to force me into anything so much as trying to guide me based on what they thought I wanted."

"They sound like amazing parents."

"They were…my mom still is," he said.

"I'm guessing by that answer there's no news about who is responsible for your father's death. I'm really sorry about that, Colton. About *all* of it."

"Before I checked the map, I was digging around in the case file. I couldn't find anything else to go on."

"Maybe no one was supposed to find him," she offered.

"It's possible. There are just so many unanswered questions. When I really focus on it, it just about drives me insane."

She could only imagine someone in his shoes, someone who was used to giving answers to others in their darkest moments, would be extremely frustrated not to be able to give those answers to his own family. She figured that between him and his brothers who worked for the US Marshal Service, they wouldn't stop until they found out why their father was killed. Their sister's kidnapping must have influenced their decisions to go into law enforcement in the first place. "How long has it been?"

"A couple of months now. He was digging around in my sister's case."

"You mentioned that she was kidnapped as a baby. Thirty-plus years is a long time. Wouldn't any leads be cold?"

"Yes. The trail was almost instantly cold and has remained so to this day. We're missing something. That's what keeps me up at night. It's the thing that I don't know yet but know is out there, which gives me nightmares. It's the one piece that, when you find it, will make the whole puzzle click together. That's been missing in my sister's case for decades."

This was the first time she'd ever heard a hint of hopelessness in Colton's voice. Despite knowing just how dangerous this path could be, she reached over and took his hand in hers. He'd done so much for her and she wanted to offer whatever reassurance she could. The electricity vibrating up her arm from their touch was something she could ignore. She needed to ignore it. Because it wasn't going to lead her down a productive path.

She couldn't agree more with Colton about timing.

"I wish there was something I could say or do to help."

"Believe it or not, just being able to talk about it for a change is nice. We never talk about Caroline's case at home. Our mother has a little gathering every year on Caroline's birthday and we have cake. She talks about what little she remembers about her daughter. It isn't much and it feels like Caroline is frozen in time. Always six months old. I've already had more time with my sons than my mother did with my sister. And I can't imagine anything happening to either one of my boys."

"It hardly seems fair," she agreed.

Colton rocked his head and twined their fingers together.

"We better get some sleep if we intend to be out the door by five thirty." He squeezed her fingers in a move that she figured was meant to be reassuring. He got up and turned off the fireplace. From the other room, he grabbed a pillow and some blankets. "For tonight, I'll take the couch."

"I thought we already talked about this." The last thing she wanted to do was steal the man's bed. It was actually a bad idea for her to think about Colton and a bed because a sensual shiver skittered across her skin.

"We did. I said I'd take the couch tonight and you'll take the bed. If I have to, I'll walk over there, pick you up and carry you to bed." At least there was a hint of lightness and playfulness in his tone now that had been missing earlier. There was also something else…something raspy in his voice when he'd mentioned his bed. And since she knew better than to tempt fate twice in one night, she pushed up to standing, walked over and gave him a peck on the cheek…and then went to bed.

COLTON SLEPT IN fifteen-minute intervals. By the time the alarm on his watch went off he'd maybe patched together an hour of sleep in seven. It was fine. He rolled off the couch and fired off a dozen pushups to get the blood pumping. He hopped to his feet and did a quick set of fifty jumping jacks. He'd been sitting way more than usual in the past thirty-six hours and his body was reminding him that it liked to be on the move.

He followed jumping jacks with sit-ups and rounded out his morning wake-up routine with squats. As quietly as he could manage, he slipped down the hall past his master bedroom, past the boys' room, where he lingered for just a second in the doorway of the open door. And then he made his way to the master bath where he washed his face, shaved and brushed his teeth.

Makena didn't need to be up for another hour. There was something right about her being curled up in his bed. He didn't need the visual, not this early in the morning. So he didn't stop off at the master bedroom on his way to the coffee machine.

The supplies were all near the machine, so he had a cup in hand and a piece of dry toast in less than three minutes. It didn't take long for the caffeine to kick in or for questions to swirl in the back of his mind.

At first, he thought about his father's case. Colton had a dedicated deputy to untangle Mrs. Hubert's financials and the contact information that had been found in her computer. Her files were all coded and his deputy was presently on full-time duty trying to crack the code. The older woman who was murdered a few months ago had ties to a kidnapping ring. Had she been involved in Caroline's case?

As a professional courtesy, and also considering the fact they were brothers, he was sharing information with Cash and Dawson. Those two were working the case in their spare time, as well. Even with a crack team of investigators, it would take time to unravel Mrs. Hubert's dealings. Time to get justice for Finn O'Connor was running out. A cold trail often led to a cold case. It occurred to Colton that his mother could be in danger, too.

There could be something hidden around the house, a file or piece of evidence their father had been hiding that could lead a perp to her door.

Colton tapped his fingers on his mug. He thought about time. And how short it could be. How unfair it could be and how quickly it could be robbed from loved ones.

It was too early in the morning to go down a path of frustration that his boys would never know their mother. Besides, as long as he had air in his lungs, he would do his best to ensure they knew what a wonderful a person she was.

Colton booted up his laptop and checked his email. Several needed attention, so he went ahead and answered those. Others could wait. A couple he forwarded on to Gert. She'd been awfully quiet since the phone call last night, which didn't mean she wasn't working. It just meant she hadn't found anything worth sharing.

He pinched the bridge of his nose to stem the headache threatening. Then he picked up the pencil from on top of his notepad. He squeezed the pencil so tight while thinking about the past that it cracked in half. Frustration that he wasn't getting anywhere in the two most important cases of his life got the best of him and he chucked the pencil pieces against the wall.

Colton cursed. He looked up in time to see a feminine figure emerge from his bedroom. Makena had on pajama bottoms and a T-shirt. The bottoms were pink plaid. Pink was his new favorite color.

"Morning." She walked into the room and right past the broken pieces of pencil.

"Back atcha." He liked that she knew where everything was and went straight to the cabinet for the coffee. She had a fresh cup in her hands and a package of vanilla yogurt by the time he moved to the spot to clean up the broken pencil.

"How'd you sleep?" he asked her as he tossed the bits into the trash.

"Like a baby." She stretched her arms out and yawned before digging into the yogurt. The movement pressed her ample breasts against the cotton of her T-shirt.

Colton forced his gaze away from her

soft curves. "How's your hip today?" He'd noticed that she was walking better and barely limped.

"So far, so good," she said. "I don't think I'm ready to run a marathon anytime soon, but I can make it across the room without too much pain. The bruise is already starting to heal." She motioned toward her hip, a place his eyes didn't need to follow.

Colton made a second cup of coffee, which he polished off by the time she finished her first.

"I can be dressed and ready in five minutes. Is that okay?" she asked.

"Works for me." He gathered up a few supplies like his notebook and laptop and tucked them into a bag.

Makena emerged from the bedroom as quickly as she'd promised, looking a little too good. He liked the fact that she could sleep when she was around him, because she'd confessed that she hadn't done a whole lot of that in recent months.

He smiled as he passed by her, taking his turn in the bedroom. He dressed in his usual jeans, dark button-down shirt and windbreaker. He retrieved his belt from the safe and then clipped it on his hip.

He returned to the kitchen where Makena stood, ready to go.

The drive to the motel took exactly twenty-nine minutes with no traffic. The place was just as Gert had described. A nondescript motel off the highway that fit the information Gert had passed along—that it rented rooms by the hour. There was an orange neon sign that had M-O-T-E-L written out along with a massive arrow pointing toward the building. Colton had always driven by those places and wondered why people needed the arrow to find it. He could chew on that another day.

"It's best if you stick to my side in case anything unexpected goes down. I'm not expecting anything, but should River still be in the area or pop in to rent another room, I want you to get behind me as a first option or anything that could put the most mass between you and him. Okay?"

She nodded and he could see that she was clear on his request. She'd been silent on the ride over, staring out the window, alone in her thoughts. Colton hadn't felt the need to fill the space between them with words. It had been a comfortable silence. One that erased the years they'd been apart.

The office of the motel was a small brick building that had a screen door in front of a white wooden one. The second door was cracked open enough to see dim lighting. He opened the screen door as he tucked Makena behind him.

With his hand on her arm, he could feel her trembling. River's connection to this place seemed to be taking a toll on her. A renewed anger filled Colton as he bit back the frustration. Of course, she'd be nervous and scared. She'd been running from this guy for literally months and here she was walking inside a building where he'd recently stayed.

Inside, they were greeted by a clerk whose head could barely be seen above the four-and-a-half-foot counter. The walls were made of dark wood paneling. The worn carpet was hunter green, and the yellow laminate countertop gave the place a leftover-from-another-era look.

"How can I help you, Sheriff?" The woman didn't seem at all surprised to see him, and he figured his deputy might've let her know someone would most likely swing by to speak to her.

"Are you Gloria?" he asked. Aside from the long bar-height counter that the little old lady could barely see over, there were a pair of chairs with a small table nestled in the right-hand side of the room. To his left, in the other corner, a flat-screen TV had been mounted.

"In the flesh." She smiled.

"I understand you spoke to one of my deputies yesterday. My name is Sheriff Colton O'Connor." He walked to the counter and extended his right hand. "Pleased to meet you."

The little old lady took his hand. Her fingers might be bony and frail but she had a solid handshake and a formidable attitude.

"Pleased to make your acquaintance, Sheriff. You're in here to talk to me about one of my clients." She had the greenest eyes he'd ever seen. He didn't get the impression she'd had an easy life. The sparkle in her eyes said she'd given it hell, though.

"Yes, ma'am. This is a friend of mine and she's familiar with the case." He purposely left out Makena's name.

Gloria nodded and smiled toward Makena. "My name might be Gloria but everyone around here calls me Peach on account of the fact I was born in Georgia. I've lived in Texas for nearly sixty years but picked up the name in second grade and it stuck."

Peach's gaze shifted back to Colton. She nodded and smiled after shaking hands with Makena.

"Can you tell me everything you remember about the visitor in room 11?" Colton asked, directing the conversation.

"The name he used to check in was Ryan Reynolds. I can get the ledger for you if you'd like to see it."

"I would." Ryan Reynolds was a famous actor, so it was obviously a fake name. Colton figured that Makena could confirm whether or not the handwriting belonged to River.

Peach opened a drawer and then produced a black book before finding a page with the date from five days ago.

"I get folks' information on the computer usually, but my cash customers like to sign in by hand the old-fashioned way." He bet they did.

She hoisted the book onto the counter and, using two fingers on each hand, nudged it toward Colton. He looked at the name she pointed at. Ryan Reynolds. The movie star. Somehow, Colton seriously doubted the real Ryan Reynolds would have come all the way to this small town to rent a motel room. Last he'd checked, there were no movies being made in the area. But this wasn't the kind of place where a person would use his or her real name, and Peach clearly hadn't asked for ID.

Colton leaned into Makena and said in a low voice, "Does that handwriting look like his?"

"Yes. He always makes that weird loop

on his Rs. I mean, wrong name, obviously. But that's his handwriting."

"Do you mind if I take a picture of this?" Colton glanced up at Peach, who nodded.

Colton pulled out his phone and snapped a shot.

"I'd also like to keep this book as evidence. Did Mr. Reynolds touch the book or use a pen that you gave him?"

"Now that I really think about it, I don't think he did touch the book. I can't be sure. But the pen he used would be right there." She reached for a decorated soup can that had a bunch of pens in it.

"If you don't mind, I'd like to admit that as evidence." Colton's words stopped her mid-reach.

"Yes, sir. I'm happy to cooperate in any way that I can."

"Thank you, ma'am." Colton tipped his chin. "Has anyone else who looked suspicious been here over the last week or two?"

"You'll have to clarify what suspicious means, sheriff. I get all kinds coming through here," she quipped with a twinkle in her eye.

Chapter Thirteen

Okay, bad question on Colton's part. "Let me ask another way. Did you have anyone new show up?"

"I have a couple of regulars who come in once a month or every other week. This is a good stop for my truckers who are on the road."

"Anyone here you haven't seen before other than Mr. Reynolds?" he clarified.

"I've had a couple of people come through. I'd say in the last week or so there've been four or five, but we've been slower than usual."

"Has anyone say around six feet tall

with light red hair, maybe could be described as strawberry blond, been in?"

She was already shaking her head before he could finish his sentence. "No. I
would remember someone like that."

"How about anyone with black hair and
a mustache?" he asked.

"No, sir." Her gaze shifted up and to
the left, signaling she was trying to recall information. So far, she'd passed his
honesty meters.

"I can't really recall anyone who looked
like that coming through recently."

"Is it possible for me to view the footage from the occupant of room 11 as he
came and went?" Colton asked.

"I can pull it up on the screen behind
you now that I have here one of those
digital files." She smiled and her eyes lit
up as she waited for his response.

"That would be a big help." Colton
turned his head and shifted slightly to
the left. He put his right elbow on the

counter, careful not to disturb the cash ledger.

The next few sounds were the click-click-clicks of fingers on a keyboard.

"Here we go," she said with an even bigger smile. "It should come up in just a second."

Colton's left hand was at his side. He felt Makena reach for him and figured she must need reassurance considering she was about to see a video of the man she'd been in a traumatic relationship with. He twined their fingers together and squeezed her hand in a show of support.

She closed what little distance was between them, her warm body against his. He ignored the frissons of heat from the contact. He'd never get used to them, but he had come to expect the reaction that always came and the warmth that flooded him while she was this close.

The TV set came to life and the sound

of static filled the room. The next thing he knew, the volume was being turned down on the set. There was a large picture window just to the left of the TV screen and Colton surveyed the parking lot of the small diner across the street. There were five vehicles: two pickup trucks, a small SUV and a sedan. He figured at least one of those had to belong to an employee, possibly two.

"Here it is. Here's the day he checked in." Peach practically beamed with her accomplishment of finding his file.

Just as Gert had explained, the video was grainy as all get-out. The man in the video wore a Rangers baseball cap and kept his chin tucked to his chest. Out of the side of his mouth, Colton asked, "Is that about his height and weight?"

"Yes." There was a lot of emotion packed in that one word and a helluva lot of fight on the ready. He couldn't help being anything but proud of her. When some would cower, she dug deep and found strength.

"I don't have a whole lot of video of him, just his coming and going." Peach fast-forwarded, pausing each time his image came into view. The time stamps revealed dates from five days ago, four days ago and three days ago. Then it was down to two days and the same thing happened every time. He'd walk in or out of the room with his chin-to-chest posture. He didn't receive any visitors during that time except for daily visits from housekeeping. He didn't come and go often, mostly staying inside. He didn't have food delivered, which meant he either packed some or went out for food once a day. His eating habits would definitely classify as strange.

And then on the last day, the morning he checked out, he did something out of character and strange. He took off his hat as he left the room and glanced up at the camera, giving the recording device a full view of his face.

Makena's body tensed and she gripped Colton's hand even tighter.

River, she'd said, was a solid six-foot-tall man with a build that made it seem like he spent serious time at the gym. He had black hair and brown eyes. And was every bit the person who'd looked straight at the camera.

From the corner of Colton's eye, he now saw a man matching the description of River exit the diner and come running at full speed toward the motel office. He put his hands in the air, palms up, in the surrender position to show that he had no gun in his hands and he was surveying the area like he expected someone to jump out at him.

MAKENA HAD NOTICED the moment she and Colton had exited the vehicle earlier that he'd rested his right hand on the butt of his gun. Having been married to someone in law enforcement, she knew exactly the reason why. It was to have instant access to his weapon. The seconds it took for his hand to reach for his gun, pull it out of the holster and shoot could mean life or death for an officer. It also reminded her of the risks they were taking by visiting the place River had been in twenty-four hours ago.

As she followed Colton's gaze, she saw her ex-husband, to the shock of her life. Her body tensed. River was running straight toward them, hands high in the air, no doubt to show that he wasn't carrying a weapon.

Colton drew his, like anyone in law enforcement would.

"Get down and stay below the counter, Ms. Peach," he directed the clerk.

He tucked Makena behind him and repositioned himself so they were behind the counter. She wanted to face River and ask him why in hell he'd tried to blow her up yesterday morning, but she wasn't stupid. She wanted to make sure she did it safely. Colton had told her to either hide behind him or put some serious mass between her and River.

She dropped Colton's hand as it went up to cup the butt of the weapon she recognized as a Glock. She glanced around, looking for some kind of weapon. There was a letter opener. She grabbed it and tightened her fist around it.

If River somehow made it past Colton to get to her, she'd be ready.

Her left hand was fisted so tightly that her knuckles went white. Anger and resentment for the way she'd had to live in the past six months bubbled up again, burning her throat.

Colton crouched so only a small portion of his head and his weapon were visible as River opened the door.

Her ex was out of breath, and the expression on his face would probably haunt her for months to come. She expected to find hurt and anger and jealousy, emotions that had been all too common during their marriage. Instead, she found panic. His eyes were wide, and he kept blinking. He was nervous.

"I swear I'm not here to hurt anyone. You have to believe me," he said. He still had that authoritative cop voice but there was a hint of fear present that was completely foreign coming from him.

"Give me one good reason we should listen to you." Colton didn't budge. "And keep your hands up where I can see them.

Colton had that same authoritative law enforcement voice that demanded attention. Hearing it from River had always caused icy fingers to grip her spine, but her body's reaction was so different when she heard it come from Colton.

All the angry words that Makena wanted

to spew at River died on her tongue. It was easy to see the man was in a panic. Whatever he'd done was catching up to him. That was her first thought.

"I swear on my mother's life that I'm not here to hurt anyone." His face was still frozen on the TV that was positioned behind him. He'd taken a couple of steps inside the room and then stopped in his tracks.

"How'd you know I was here?" Makena asked.

"I saw you come in, and they will, too," came the chilling response.

"Who are *they*?" Colton asked.

"I can't tell you and you don't want to know. Believe me. The only thing you need to be aware of is that your life is in danger." River's voice shook with dread and probably a shot of adrenaline.

A half-mirthful, half-frustrated sigh shot from Makena's throat. He wasn't telling her anything she didn't already know.

Makena locked eyes with the terri-
fied older woman at the other end of
the counter. Peach kept eye contact with
Makena when she pointed at something
inside a shelf. It was hidden from view
and Makena had a feeling it was some
kind of weapon, like a bat or a shotgun.

Makena shook her head. Peach nodded
and tilted her head toward it.

"Talk to me, River. Tell me why they
would be after me. Is it because of you?"
As much as Makena didn't believe that
anymore, she had to ask. She needed to
hear from him that wasn't the case, and
she needed to get him talking so she
could understand why it seemed like the
world was crumbling around her.

"It's not important *what* you know. It's
what they *think* you know. Even more
important right now is that you get the
hell out of here. Stay low. Stick with this
guy." He motioned toward Colton. "He
can probably protect you if you stay out

of sight. Just give me time. I need time to straighten everything out."

"Time? To what? Plant another bomb?" she said.

She'd never seen River look this rattled before. And also…something else…helpless? His eyes darted around the room and he looked like he'd jump out of his skin if a cat hopped up on the counter.

This close, she could see his bloodshot eyes and the dark circles underneath. They always got that way when he went days without sleep. He was almost in a manic state and part of her wondered if deep down he actually did care about her well-being or if this was all some type of self-preservation act. To make it seem like he was a victim. But to what end?

"I knew they were planning something, but I had no idea…" River brought his hands on top of his head. His face distorted. "Everything's a mess now. I made everything a mess. I never meant for you to get caught up in this. Bad timing. But just do what I say and lie low. Trust me, you don't want to get anywhere near these guys."

His words sent another cold chill racing down her spine.

"You're not getting off that easy, River," Colton said. "Start talking now. I can work with the DA. I can talk with your chief if you give me something to take to him."

River's emotions were escalating, based on the increasing intensity of his expression.

This was not good. This was so not good.

"Are you kidding me right now? It's too late for me. It's too late to go back and fix what's wrong. I messed up big-time. There's not going to be any coming back from this for me but there's still time for me to fix it for you."

"Hold on. Just do me a favor and slow

down." Colton's deep voice was a study in calm. "This doesn't have to end badly. Whatever you've done… I can't promise any miracles, but I can say that I'll do everything in my power if you talk. You need to tell us what's going on. You need to tell us who those men are and exactly why they're after Makena. It's the only way that I can help you."

River seemed more agitated. "You just don't understand. You don't get this and you don't realize what I'm going through or what I've done. It's too late. It's too late for me. I can accept that. But not her. She didn't do anything wrong."

The fact that River was concerned about her when it appeared his own life was on the line told her that she hadn't married a 100 percent jerk all those years ago. There had been something good inside him then and maybe she could work with that now.

Makena stood up taller so that she could

look River in the eye, hoping that would make a difference. "I don't know what happened, River. But I do know there was a decent person in there at one time. The person I first met—"

"Is gone. That guy is long gone. Forget about the past and forget that you ever knew me. Just lie low and give me some time to get this straightened out."

"I've been in hiding for half a year, River. How much more of my life do I need to give up for whatever you did?" she asked.

Instead of calming him, that seemed to rile him up even more. She'd been truthful and her words seemed to have the effect of punching him.

"I know, Makena. I realize that none of this makes sense to you, and it's best for everyone else if it doesn't. If I could go back and change things, I would. Time doesn't work like that and our past mistakes do come back to haunt us."

Makena remembered that he was on leave for some pretty hefty charges. Maybe if she pretended like she already knew, he would come clean. "The men who are after me, who tried to blow me up…are they related to your administrative leave?"

River issued a sharp sigh and then started lowering his hands.

"Keep 'em up, high and where I can see them." Colton's voice left no room for doubt that he was not playing around. He could place River under arrest, she knew, but he seemed to be holding off long enough to get answers. She took it as a sign he believed River might give them useful information.

River's hands shot up in the air. Being in law enforcement, he would be very aware just how serious Colton was about those words. Colton's department-issued Glock was still aimed directly at River.

All it would take was one squeeze of the trigger to end River's life.

Considering the man was standing not ten feet away, Colton wouldn't need a crackerjack shot to take him out.

"What did you do, River?" Makena asked again, hoping to wear him down and get answers. "You can help me the most if you tell Colton what you're involved in."

Hands in the air, River started pacing. He appeared more agitated with every forward step. His mood was dangerous and volatile. Deadly?

She scanned his body for signs of a weapon, knowing full well there had to be one there somewhere. On duty, he'd worn an ankle holster. It wasn't uncommon for him to hide his Glock in another holster tucked in the waistband of his jeans.

He mumbled and she couldn't make out what he was saying. And then he spun around to face them. "Did you say his name is Colton?"

"Yes, but I don't see how that has any bearing on anything."

"Really? Isn't that your ex-boyfriend from college? I used to read your journals, Makena."

Her face burned with a mix of embarrassment and outrage. She hadn't kept a journal since their early years of marriage. And yes, she had probably written something in it about Colton. But it had been so long ago she couldn't remember what she'd written.

"Colton was never my boyfriend. He wasn't then and he isn't now. But even if he was, that's none of your business anymore. In case you forgot, we're divorced. And this is my life, a life that I want back." She'd allowed him to take so much time of hers. No more.

Makena took in a deep breath because the current assertiveness, although she deserved to stand up for herself, wasn't exactly having a calming effect on River.

In fact, she feared she might be making it worse. She willed her nerves to calm down and her stress levels to relax.

"I won't pretend to know what you're going through right now." Colton's voice was a welcome calm in the eye of the storm. "I know you're facing some charges at work but if you help in this case it'll be noted in your jacket. It won't hurt and might convince a jury to go easier on you."

River looked at Colton. His gaze bounced back to Makena.

"Man, it's too late for me now."

And then the sound of a bullet split the air, followed by glass breaking on the front door.

The next few minutes happened in slow motion. Out of the corner of her eye, Makena saw Peach reach into the shelf. The older woman came up with a shotgun in a movement that was swift and efficient. It became pretty obvious this wasn't the woman's first rodeo.

She aimed the barrel of the gun right at River. But it was River who caught and held Makena's attention. As she ducked for cover, the look on his face would be etched in her brain forever.

At first his eyes bulged, and he took a step forward. She could've sworn she heard something whiz past her ear and was certain it was a second bullet. Before she realized, Colton positioned his body in between her and River.

River's arms dropped straight out. His chest flew toward her as he puffed it out. It was then she saw the red dot flowering in the center of his white cotton T-shirt. His mouth flew open, forming a word that never came out.

Shock stamped his features. He looked down at the center of his chest and said, "I've been shot."

He looked up at Makena and then Colton before repeating the words.

Colton was already on the radio clipped to his shoulder, saying words that would stick in her mind for a long time. She heard phrases like "officer down" and "ambulance required." This was all a little too real as she saw a pair of men, side by side and weapons at the ready, making their way across the street and toward the motel.

"I have to get you out of here," Colton said to Makena. The truck was parked behind the motel and she saw the brilliance of his plan now.

"Okay." It was pretty much the only word she could form or manage to get out under the circumstances. And then more came. "What about River?"

"There's nothing we can do to help him right now. The best thing we can do is lead those men away from the motel."

Colton turned to Peach. "Is the back door locked?"

"Yes, sir." She ran a hand along the shelf and produced a set of keys. She tossed them to Colton, who snatched them with one hand. "You need to come with us. It's not safe here."

Peach lowered her face to the eyepiece of the shotgun. "I'll hold 'em off. You two get out of here while you can. I'll hold down the fort."

"I'm not kidding, Peach. You need to come with us now."

The woman shook her head and that was as much as she said.

"Help is on the way," Colton shouted to River, who'd taken a few steps back and dropped against the door, closing it. He sat with a dumbfounded look on his face.

"Reach up and lock that," Peach shouted to him.

Surprisingly, he obliged.

"We have to go." Colton, with keys in

one hand and a Glock in the other, offered an arm, which Makena took as they ran toward the back.

He unlocked a key-only dead bolt and then tossed the keys into the hallway before fishing his own keys out of his pocket. The two of them ran toward the truck, which was thankfully only a few spaces from the door.

Once inside, he cranked on the ignition and backed out of the parking spot. "Stay low. Keep your head down. It's best if you get down on the floorboard."

Makena did as he requested. She noticed he'd scooted down, making himself as small as possible and less visible, therefore less of a target. He put the vehicle into Drive and floored the gas pedal.

In a ball on the floorboard as directed, Makena took in a sharp breath as Colton jerked the truck forward. It was a big vehicle and not exactly nimble. Size was its best asset.

"They have no idea who they're dealing with," Colton commented, and she realized it was because they were in his personal vehicle and not one marked as law enforcement.

A crack of a bullet split the air. It was then that Makena heard the third shot being fired.

Chapter Fourteen

Colton tilted his chin toward his left shoulder where his radio was clipped on his jacket. His weapon was in the hand that he also used to steer the wheel after they'd bolted from around the back of the motel.

Peach would be safe as he drew the perps away from the building and onto the highway. River had been shot and it looked bad for him, but he was still talking and alert, and that was a good sign.

Getting Makena out of the building and Birchwood had been his first priority. River was right about one thing. She'd be safer if she kept a low profile.

Colton also realized the reason the perps were shooting was probably because they didn't realize they were shooting at a sheriff. Even so, it had been one of his better ideas to slip out the back of his office yesterday and take his personal vehicle, because it seemed as though the perps had zeroed in on Makena's location at the RV.

They also seemed ready and able to shoot River though he was an officer of the law. With River's professional reputation tarnished, plus the charges being lobbed against him, they must think they could get away with shooting him.

"Gert, can you read me?" He hoped like hell she could, because she was his best link to getting help for River and for him and Makena.

Birchwood was in Colton's jurisdiction. One of his deputies passed by this motel on his daily drive to work, and Colton hoped that he was nearby, possibly on his way into work.

Gert's voice came through the radio. "I read you loud and clear."

"I have two perps who have opened fire on my personal vehicle. And an officer is down at the motel. Makena is in my custody and we're heading toward the station, coming in hot."

"Do you have a vehicle or a license plate or can you give me anything on who might be behind you?"

"The shooter was on foot." Colton took a moment to glance into his rearview mirror in time to see the pair of perps running toward a Jeep.

With the weight of his truck, he didn't have a great chance of outrunning them. "It's looking like a Jeep Wrangler. White. Rubicon written in black letters on the hood. I don't have a license plate but I imagine it won't take them long to catch up to me. If they have one on the front of their vehicle, I can relay it."

He heard Makena suck in a breath. She scrambled into the seat and practically glued her face to the back window. "What can I do?"

"Stay low. Stay hidden. I don't have a way to identify myself in the truck. My vehicle is slow. But I'm going to do my level best to outrun them."

Makena didn't respond, so he wasn't certain she bought into his request. He was kicking up gravel on the service road to the four-lane highway. He took the first entrance ramp, and despite it being past seven o'clock in the morning on a Friday, there were more cars than he liked.

"Where are they now?" Makena asked.

"They're making their way toward us on the service road." Colton swerved in and out of the light traffic, pressing his dual cab truck to its limits. What it lacked in get-up-and-go, it made up for in size. If nothing else, he'd use its heft to block the Jeep from pulling alongside them.

Of course, the passenger could easily get off a shot from behind.

Colton leaned his mouth to his shoulder. "Where's the nearest marked vehicle?"

"Not close enough. I'm checking on DPS now to see if I can get a trooper in your direction. How are you doing? Can you hold them off until I can get backup to you?"

"I don't have a choice." Colton meant those words.

The Jeep had taken the on-ramp onto the highway and it wouldn't be long before it was on his bumper. He glanced around at the traffic and figured he'd better take this fight off the highway rather than endanger innocent citizens.

River was in trouble at work. Colton

knew that for certain. What he wasn't sure of was his partners.

Colton relayed the description of the perps to Gert. "Call Chief Shelton at Dallas PD and see if any of his officers matching those descriptions have been connected in any way to River Myers. I want to know who River's friends were. Who he hung out with in the department and if any of them had visited the shooting range lately."

Most beat cops couldn't pull off the shot Red had at that distance and through a glass door. Whoever made the shot would get high scores in marksmanship at the range. Other officers would take note. Someone would know.

Between that and the physical descriptions, maybe River's supervising officer could narrow the search.

"Hold on, I'm going to swerve off the highway," he said, noting his chance.

At the last minute, he cranked the

steering wheel right and made the exit ramp. It was probably too much to hope the perps lost him in traffic. There were plenty of black trucks on these roads.

He cursed when the Jeep took the exit.

"Gert, talk to me. Do you have someone at the motel?" Colton's only sense of relief so far was that he'd drawn the perps away from Peach and River. He also had a sneaky suspicion that Peach could take care of herself and could keep River there at gunpoint. Colton had no doubt the woman could hold her own until River received medical attention.

He could only hope that River would come clean with names.

Again, all they needed was a puzzle piece. At least now they knew that River had some connection to Red and Mustache. There was something the three of them had concocted or were doing they believed would land them in jail if someone found out. That someone, unfortunately, ended up being Makena. And again, he was reminded of how timing was everything.

If Makena had gone out to that garage five minutes before, maybe the men wouldn't have been there yet. Maybe River could've convinced her to go back to bed and she could be living out a peaceful life by now after the divorce.

His mind stretched way back to college. He'd wanted to ask her out but hadn't. Again, the ripple effect of that decision caused him to wonder about his timing. Now was not the time to dredge up the past. Besides, the Jeep was gaining on him. At this pace, it would catch him.

There were fields everywhere. One was a pasture for grazing. The other was corn stalks. The truck could handle either one and so could the Jeep. Colton couldn't get any advantage by veering off road. Except that in the corn, considering it was already tall, maybe he could lose them.

The meadow on the other side of the street was useless. The last thing he needed was more flat land. And while he didn't like the idea of damaging someone's crop and potential livelihood, he knew that he could circle back and make restitution. What was the point of having a trust fund he'd never touched if not for a circumstance like this one?

"Hang on tight, okay?" he said to Makena.

When she confirmed, he nailed a hard right. The truck bounded so hard he thought he might've cracked the chassis but stabilized once he got onto the field. The last thing he saw was the Jeep following.

Colton's best chance to confuse them was to maybe do a couple of figure eights and then zigzag through the cornfield. It would at the very least keep the perps from getting off a good shot. He was running out of options.

So far, the Jeep hadn't gotten close enough to them for him to be able to read a license plate if there was one on the front. Law required it to be there. However, many folks ignored it.

Considering these guys had good reason to hide any identifying marks, they most certainly wouldn't have a plate up front.

Gert's voice cut through his thoughts. "I got you pulled up on GPS using your cell phone. I have a location on you, sir. Can you hold tight in the area until I can get someone to you?"

"That's affirmative. I can stick around as long as I keep moving." He tried to come off as flippant so Gert wouldn't worry about him any more than she already was.

Makena was getting bounced around in the floorboard. At this point, it would be safer for her to climb into the seat and strap in. So that was exactly what he told her to do.

She managed, without being thrown around too much.

The crops had the truck bouncing and slowed his speed considerably. He cut a few sharp turns, left and then right... right and then left. A couple of figure eights.

There was a time in his life when a ride like this might've felt exciting. His adrenaline was pumping and he'd be all in for the thrill. Even having a couple of idiots with guns behind him would've seemed like a good challenge. A lot had changed in him after he'd become a dad last year.

He took life more seriously and especially his own. Because he knew without a shadow of a doubt those boys needed their father to come home every night. And he would, today, too.

He checked his mirrors and was feeling pretty good about where he stood with regard to the perps. Until he almost slammed into the Jeep that had cut an angle right in front of him.

Slamming the brake and narrowly avoiding a collision, Colton bit out a few choice words.

Gert's voice came across the radio again. "Sir, I have names. Officer Randol Bic and Officer Jimmy Stitch were known associates of River Myers and fit the descriptions you gave. Bic is a sharpshooter. They're partners in East Dallas and both of their records are clean."

A picture was emerging. Was River taking the fall for Bic and Stitch?

Had they threatened him? Were they holding something over his head?

"I've heard those names before," Makena said.

Gert's voice came across the radio. "Sir, I think the GPS is messing up. It looks like you're driving back and forth on the highway."

Colton couldn't help himself; he laughed. "Well, that's because I'm presently driving in a cornfield near the highway. GPS probably can't register that location."

"I feel like I should have known it would be something like that." Now Gert laughed. It was good to break up some of the tension. A sense of humor helped with keeping a calm head, which could be the difference between making a mistake or a good decision.

The Jeep circled back, and Colton could hear its engine gunning toward him. He cut left, trying to outrun the perps.

"Gert, how are you doing over there?" Colton needed an update. Actually, what he needed was a miracle. But he'd stopped believing in those after losing Rebecca, and he figured it was best to keep his feet firmly planted on the ground and his head out of the clouds.

"Sir, I have good news for you. Do you hear anything?"

Colton strained to listen. He didn't hear anything other than the sound of his front bumper hacking through the cornfield. He hated to think what he was doing to this farmer's crops. But again, he would pay restitution.

"I don't hear much more than the noise I'm making and the sound of an engine barreling toward me." He was barely cutting around.

The Jeep was close, he could hear and feel it, if not see it.

"Well, sir, the cavalry is arriving. If you roll your window down, I think you'll be happy with what you hear. DPS got back to me and a trooper should be on top of you right now."

Well, maybe Colton had been too quick to write off the likelihood of miracles happening.

"That's the best news I've heard all

day." When he really listened and got past the sounds of corn husks slapping against his front bumper, he heard the familiar wails of sirens in the distance.

Makena was practically glued to her seat, with her hands gripping the strap of her seat belt.

"If you like that news, I've got more. An ambulance is en route to the motel. Help is on the way, sir."

"Gert, remind me the next time I see you that you deserve a raise."

"Sir, I'm going to hold you to that when it's time for my review." Again, lightening the tension with teasing kept his mind at ease and his brain able to focus. The minute he thought a situation was the end of the world was the minute it would be true.

Colton circled around a few more times, ensuring that he was on the move and as far away from the Jeep as possible. He figured the perps had probably given up once they'd heard sirens.

Since they were cops with clean records, they would want to keep them that way. When he really thought about it, they'd concocted the perfect scenario. The puzzle pieces clicked together in one moment.

They had some type of hold over River. That was obvious and a given. They believed that Makena could possibly link them to River and so they would get rid of her. All the while implicating River, who was already known to have a temper and a bad relationship with his wife.

When the different parts of their plan made sense like that, he realized the genius of their plot. However, he had seen them. He knew who they were. That was where they'd messed up. Now they'd gone and left a trail.

"Are they gone?" Makena looked around as Colton slowed down.

"I believe so."

Makena sank back in the chair. "I hear the sirens."

Colton nodded as he tried to navigate back toward the highway.

"I can patch you through to Officer Staten," Gert said.

"Ten-four. Great work, Gert." But before Colton could speak to the highway patrolman through the radio, he saw the cruiser. Colton flashed his headlights and cut off his engine.

Hands up, he exited his truck and told Makena to do the same.

After greeting Officer Staten, Colton said, "It's a shame I didn't get a plate. A white Jeep Rubicon in Texas doesn't exactly stand out."

"The two of you are safe. That's the most important thing to me right now," Officer Staten said.

There was no arguing with that point.

"Do you need assistance getting back

to your office?" Staten was tall and darker-skinned, with black hair, brown eyes and a deceptively lean frame. Every state trooper could pull his own weight and more in a fight. These officers traveled long distances with no backup in sight. To say they were tough was a lot like saying Dwayne Johnson had a few muscles.

Colton looked to Makena. "Any chance I can convince you to take a ride back to my office with the officer?"

Makena was already vigorously shaking her head before he could finish his sentence. He figured as much. It was worth a try. He wanted her to be safely tucked away while he circled back and checked on River and Peach.

She seemed to read his mind when she said, "I'm going with you."

There was so much determination in her voice he knew better than to argue. No use wasting precious time.

Colton turned to Officer Staten and said, "Can I get an assist to the motel where an officer was fired on? I'd like to go back and investigate the scene. And considering I have a witness with me, I think it might be best if I have backup."

Staten seemed to catch on, because he was already nodding. "I'm happy to help in any way I can."

Professional courtesy went a long way and Colton had gone to great lengths to build a cooperative relationship with other law enforcement agencies.

Once their destination was agreed upon, Colton retreated to his truck with Makena by his side.

The drive back to the motel surprisingly took half an hour. Colton didn't realize they'd gotten so far from the motel, but then he was driving back at normal speed limits, whereas he'd flown to get away from there.

There was a BOLO out on the Jeep.

If they were as smart as they appeared to be, they would ditch the vehicle. The new problem was that they'd been made and now they had nothing to lose. Dangerous.

They couldn't possibly realize that Colton had figured out who they were. So Colton had that on his side.

By the time they reached the motel, it looked like a proper crime scene. An ambulance was there. The back had been closed up and it looked as though they were about to pull away.

"Hold on a sec," Colton said to Makena.

He hopped out of his pickup, knowing that Makena would want to know River's status.

He jogged up to the driver's side of the ambulance and the driver rolled down the window. Fortunately for him, he still had on his windbreaker that had the word SHERIFF in big bold letters running down his left sleeve, so it was easy to identify that he was in law enforcement.

"How is your patient in the back?" Colton asked. "I was here at the time of the shooting. I had to get a witness out of the building. What is the status of your patient?"

"GSW to the back, exit wounds in his chest. We need to rock and roll, sir. No guarantees on this one. Still breathing, but a lot of blood loss by the time we got here."

Colton took a step back and waved them on. "Go."

It wasn't good news, but River was still alive and Colton had learned that even a tiny bit of hope was better than none. As done as Makena was with the relationship, and he had no doubt in his mind the marriage had been over for a very long time, she was the type of person to be concerned for someone she'd once cared about.

He wished he could give her better news.

Glancing toward the truck, he expected to see her waiting there. A moment of shock jolted him when he saw that she was gone. Then, he knew immediately where she would go. He raced inside to see her standing next to Peach, who was sitting in one of the chairs on the right-hand side.

Makena was offering reassurances to the older woman while rubbing her shoulders. Peach had blood all over her flowery dress.

"I did everything I could to help him, but there was so much blood. He was already pale by the time we got help. His lips were turning blue." The anguish in the older woman's voice was palpable.

"Peach, what you did was admirable. If he has any chance at all, it's because of you," Colton said.

Peach glanced up at him, those emerald green eyes sparkling with gratitude for his comments.

"I mean it. You very well could've saved his life here and I know you saved ours. I would work beside you in law enforcement any day." He meant every word.

Her chin lifted with his praise.

"I appreciate your saying so, Sheriff. It means a lot."

Colton crouched down to eye level with her before taking her statement. And then Makena took Peach into a back room where she washed up.

Makena stayed by the elderly woman's side long after the blood had been rinsed off and Peach had changed clothes.

The highway patrolman stayed outside, guarding the front door in case the perps returned. The front door was cordoned off with crime scene tape.

"My deputy here is going to process the scene. Can one of us give you a ride home?" Colton asked Peach.

"I'll be all right in a few minutes," Peach said. Her hands had steadied. "I have my car out back and I don't want to leave it here overnight."

"What's the owner's name? I'll give 'em a call and ask for someone to cover your shift."

Whatever he said seemed to tickle Peach.

"You're looking at the owner. I owned this place with my husband, God rest his soul."

"Can I call someone? It's not a good idea for you to be alone right now." The shock of what had happened would wear off and her emotions could sneak up on her. Colton didn't want her to suffer. She'd shown incredible bravery today.

"I have a daughter in town," she said. "I'll see if she'll make up the guest bedroom for me tonight."

"Any chance you could get her on the phone now?" Colton asked.

"My purse is underneath the counter where Rapture was hiding." She motioned toward her shotgun that was sitting on top of the counter. It had been opened and the shells looked to have been removed.

As he waited for Peach to call her daughter, Colton took stock of the situation. He now had names. He had motive. All he needed was opportunity to seal Bic and Stitch's fate.

Chapter Fifteen

Makena heard Colton's voice as she sat with Peach. He was talking about shock and the need to keep an eye on her. The concern in his voice brought out all kinds of emotions in Makena. She could tell that he genuinely cared about Peach and it was just about the kindest thing Makena thought she'd ever witnessed. But that was just Colton. He was genuine, kind and considerate wrapped in a devastatingly handsome and masculine package. There was nothing self-centered about him. In fact, there was a sad quality in his eyes that made him so real.

"Bernard and I spent our whole lives here at this motel. He never would take a vacation. I used to tease him about what he'd turn into with all work and no play." A wistful and loving look overtook Peach's face when she spoke about her husband.

"He sounds like an honest, hard-working man," Makena said.

"That he was. He was good to me and I was good to him. We had two daughters. One who succumbed to illness as a child, and the other who your boyfriend is on the phone with now. She looks after me. She's been on me to sell the business for years." Peach exhaled. "It's difficult to let go. Here is where I feel Bernard's presence the most. I always thought I'd start a little restaurant. Even had a name picked out, but I never did find the time. I always would rather be feeding people. The motel was Bernard's baby."

The fact that Peach had referred to

Colton as Makena's boyfriend didn't get past her. She didn't see this as the time to correct the elderly woman.

She glanced up, and it was then that the flat-screen TV caught her attention. She remembered the date stamp and the time stamp on the screen when River had looked up. He'd looked up at exactly 6:12 a.m., which meant he was at the motel and not anywhere near Katy Gulch and he must have known something was going to happen even if he didn't know what because he'd given himself an alibi. Birchwood was a solid half hour from town. He'd been inside his room the entire night, based on the camera footage. The only window was in front, next to the door. If he'd tried to climb out, the camera would've picked it up.

As far as she knew there were no other exits in the room, which pretty much ensured that he was innocent.

A flood of relief washed over her that he hadn't been involved in the bombing attempt. Bic and Stitch's whereabouts had yet to be known, and she had plenty of questions for the pair.

Makena sat with her hands folded in her lap. She refocused on the story Peach was telling her about how her beloved Bernard had singlehandedly patched up a roof after a tornado. Peach was rambling and Makena didn't mind. The woman's smooth, steady voice had a calming effect, and she figured Peach needed to keep her mind busy by talking.

Colton stepped back into the room and then handed the phone to Peach, who took it and spoke to her daughter.

While Peach was occupied, Makena motioned for Colton to come closer. He bent down and took a knee beside her. She liked that he immediately reached for her hand. She leaned toward his ear and relayed her discovery.

He rocked his head. "That's a really good point. If he was here all night, he couldn't have been the one to set the bomb. We have two names, and their department will want to be involved. I promise you here and now justice will be served."

Makena hoped he could deliver on that promise before they could get to her. Bic and Stitch had proven they'd go to any length to quiet her.

"I already figured out they were setting River up. It's a pretty perfect setup and that's the reason we found the black key chain at the scene." After everything she'd been through with River, she probably shouldn't care one way or the other about it. She just wasn't built that way. She did care. Not just about him but about anyone who'd taken a wrong turn.

"Any chance we can stop by the hospital when we leave here?" Makena asked.

"I think that can be arranged."

She really hoped so, because she wanted to see with her own eyes that River was okay.

"Since we know he's a target, will there be security? How will that work?" she asked.

"I just called in a report that he's a material witness in an attempted murder case. One of my deputies is with him and we'll make sure he's not left unattended in the hospital while he fights for his life." Colton's words were reassuring.

"Excuse me, sir." Trooper Staten stepped inside the room.

"How can I help you?"

"Since you have a deputy here, I'd like to offer backup to one of my buddies who has a trucker pulled over not far from here. If you think you'll be good without me, I'd like to assist."

"We're good. Thank you for everything. Your help is much appreciated."

Colton stood up, crossed the room and shook the state trooper's hand.

Deputy Fletcher worked to process the scene while Colton and Makena waited for Peach's daughter to show. She did, about twenty minutes later. The young woman, who looked to be in her late twenties, had a baby on her hip and a distressed look on her face as she approached the motel.

Rather than let her step into the bloody scene before it could be cleaned up, Colton met her at the door. He turned back in time to say, "Makena, do you want to bring Peach outside?"

"Sure. No problem." She helped Peach to her feet.

The older woman gripped Makena's arm tightly and it gave her the impression Peach was holding on for dear life. It was good that her daughter was picking her up. She needed someone to take care of her.

Seeing the look on her daughter's face as soon as they stepped outside sent warmth spreading through Makena. The mother-daughter bond hit her square in the chest, and for the first time, Makena thought she was missing out on something by not having a child of her own.

When Peach was settled in her daughter's small SUV and the baby had been strapped in the back seat, the older woman looked up with weary eyes.

"Maybe it is a good idea for me to sell. My handyman, Ralph, can keep things running until the sale. He can see to it if anyone needs a rental. You were right to have me call my daughter," she said to Colton. "Good luck with everything. Take care of yourselves." Peach glanced from Makena to Colton and back. "And take care of each other. If you don't mind my saying, the two of you have something special. That's probably the most important thing you can have in life."

"Thank you, ma'am," Colton said.

Again, Makena didn't see the need to correct Peach despite the thrill of hope she felt at hearing those words. Peach had been through a traumatic experience and Makena wasn't going to ruin her romantic notions by clarifying her relationship with Colton. He had become her lifeline and that was most likely the reason the thought of being separated from him at some point gave her heart palpitations, not that she'd reactivated real feelings for him. The kind of feelings that could go the distance.

COLTON CHECKED HIS WATCH. He surveyed the area, well aware that it had only been a short while ago that two perps had been walking across that same street.

A second deputy pulled up. Colton motioned for him to go on inside. He didn't want anyone working alone on this scene or this case.

He turned to Makena. "River is probably still in surgery. Do you think you could eat something?"

Peach wasn't the only one in shock. Makena was handling hers well, but she'd had months of being on the run and hiding to practice dealing with extreme emotions.

Makena closed the distance between them and leaned against him.

Colton looped his arms around her waist and pulled her body flush with his. This time, he was the one who dipped his head and pressed a kiss to her lips. He told himself he did it to root them both in reality again, but there was so much more to it, to being with her.

The thought of how close he'd come to losing her sent a shiver rocketing down his back. He'd lost enough with Rebecca and he didn't want to lose another friend.

Makena took in a deep breath. "How do you think he knew?"

Colton knew exactly what she was talking about. She was picking up their conversational thread from a few minutes ago.

"It's possible he didn't. It's likely he assumed that something could happen. He might have followed them here. Maybe they disappeared for a couple of days, and he realized they were searching for you and had found you. So he must've decided following them was his best chance at finding you. You were the wild card. They had no idea when you were going to show up and what evidence you might bring with you. They've probably been looking for you this entire time, and the fact that you disappeared when you did made it look that much more like you had something to hide or fear."

"Timing," she said on another sigh. It was a loaded word.

She blinked up at him and those crystal clear blue eyes brought out feelings he hadn't felt since college. He had no idea what to do with them. Complicated didn't begin to describe their lives. But he liked her standing right where she was, her warm body pressed against his and his arms circling her waist.

Colton glanced around, surveying the area. Even with two deputies on-site he couldn't let his guard down.

"What do you say we eat at the cafeteria in the hospital?" Makena asked.

"I need to let these guys know where we're headed and communicate with Gert so she can keep someone close to us." Traveling this way was cumbersome and frustrating. An idea sparked. He twined his and Makena's fingers before walking back inside the building. "How about one of you gentlemen lend me your service vehicle? I can leave my truck here. I don't want either one of you driving it.

I'll have it towed back to my office. And then the two of you can buddy up on the way back to the office, where you can pick up another vehicle."

Both of his deputies were already nodding their agreement.

Deputy Fletcher pitched a set of keys to Colton, which he caught with one hand. He figured that he and Makena would be a helluva lot safer in a marked vehicle than his truck. Not to mention Bic and Stitch knew exactly what he drove. They may have even pulled some strings and run the plates by now, which would work in Colton's favor. He highly doubted they would've shot at a sheriff if they'd known.

Colton led Makena out to the county-issued SUV.

The drive to the hospital was forty minutes long. Colton located a parking spot as close to the ER doors as he could find. He linked his and Makena's fingers before walking into the ER bay. He was ever aware that a sharpshooter could be anywhere, waiting to strike. But what he hoped was that Bic and Stitch had gone back to Dallas to regroup.

Now that their chief was aware, they would be brought in for questioning. It would have to be handled delicately. Their plan to set up River had blown up in their faces, as had their plans to erase Makena.

The strangest part about the whole thing was that they were targeting her based on what they thought she knew, while she really knew nothing. But now Dallas P.D and the sheriff's office knew what the men were capable of.

On the annual summer barbecue night, Colton and his staff would sit around a campfire way too late and swap stories. Conversation always seemed to drift toward what everyone would do if it went down, meaning they had to disappear.

The first thing people said was obvious. Get rid of their cell phone. The next was that they'd stay the heck away from their personal vehicle. Another thing was not to go home again. That seemed obvious. Most of the deputies said they'd go to the ATM and withdraw as much money as they could before heading to Mexico. At least one said she would head toward Canada because she thought it was the opposite way anyone would look for her.

Bic and Stitch had to have a backup plan. It was just a cop's instinct to talk through worst-case scenarios. And if they thought like typical cops, like he was certain they did considering they had twenty-six years of police experience between them, he figured they had an escape plan, too.

So the thought of them going back to their homes or to Dallas was scratched. Their cover was blown.

But did they realize it?

One thing was certain: they didn't have anything to gain sticking around town. In fact, it would do them both good to hide out until this blew over. And then take off for the border.

What would their escape plan be? He wondered where they'd been hiding while River booked the motel room.

It was a lot to think about. Colton needed a jolt of caffeine and he probably needed something in his stomach besides acid from coffee. The piece of toast he'd had for breakfast wasn't holding up anymore.

He stopped off at the nurses' station in the ER.

"Can you point me to the cafeteria?" It wouldn't do any good to ask about River yet and these women most likely wouldn't know. He would go to the information desk, which would be in the front lobby.

"Straight down this hallway, make a right and then a left. You'll find a lobby, which you'll need to cross. You'll get to a hallway on the exact opposite side and you'll want to take that. You can't miss it from there."

Colton thanked the intake nurse and then followed her directions to a T. A minute later, they were standing in front of a row of vending machines that had everything from hot chocolate to hot dogs.

"Does any of this look appetizing?" he asked Makena.

She walked slowly, skimming the contents of each vending machine. She stopped at the third one and then pointed. "I think this ham sandwich could work."

Colton bought two of them, then grabbed a couple bags of chips. She wanted a soft drink while he stuck with black coffee.

There was a small room with a few

bright orange plastic tables and chairs scattered around the room. Each table had from three to six chairs surrounding it. There were two individuals sitting at different tables, each staring at their phone.

Makena took the lead and chose a table farthest away from the others. The sun was shining, and hours had passed since breakfast.

"So I noticed you didn't ask about River." Makena took a bite and chewed on her ham sandwich.

"No, the intake nurses either wouldn't have information or wouldn't share it. There's an information desk we can stop at after we eat. I know most of the people who work there and figured that would be the best place to check his status" He checked his smartwatch. "Gert would let me know if the worst had happened, if River had died."

"Have you given much thought to what

your life might look like once this is all behind you?" Colton asked Makena after they'd finished eating.

"Every day for the past six months I've thought about what I would do once this was all over. To be honest, I never really had an answer that stuck. I went through phases. One of those phases was to just buy a little farmhouse somewhere away from people and live on my own and maybe get a golden retriever for company."

"There are worse ways to spend your life."

She smiled and continued. "Then, I had a phase where I wanted to move far away from Texas and live in a major metropolitan area where there would be people everywhere, but no one would bother me unless I wanted them to. If I wanted to be left alone, people would respect that. But I would be around life again. I'd be around people doing things and being busy. I wouldn't have to hide my face." She looked out the window thoughtfully. "None of those things stuck for more than a month."

"And how about now?"

"I have a few ideas." She turned to face him and looked him in the eyes. "Now I feel like I know what I want, but that maybe it's out of reach."

Before he could respond, a text came in from Gert that River was out of surgery. Gert had connections in most places and the hospital was no different. Glancing at his watch, he realized an hour had passed since they'd arrived at the hospital.

Colton made a mental note to finish this conversation later, because a very large part of him wanted to know if she saw any chance of the two of them spending time together. It was pretty much impossible for him to think about starting a new relationship while he had one-year-old twins at home, especially with what was going on with his family.

His mind came up with a dozen reasons straight out of the chute as to why it was impossible and wouldn't happen and could never go anywhere. Why he couldn't risk it.

But the heart didn't listen to logic. It wanted to get to know Makena again. To see if the fire in the kisses they'd shared— kisses he was having one helluva time trying to erase from his memory—could ignite something that might last longer than a few months.

Logic flew out the window when it came to the heart.

"River is out of surgery and I can probably get us up to his floor if not his room."

Makena looked like she wanted to say something and then thought better of it.

"Let's do it." She took in a sharp breath,

like she was steadying herself for what she knew would come.

Colton cursed the timing of the text, but it was good news. He led them to the information desk where he could get details about which floor River was housed in. Trudy, a middle-aged single mother who lived on the outskirts of Katy Gulch, sat at the counter.

As sheriff, Colton liked to get to know his residents and look out for those who seemed to need it. Trudy had been widowed while her husband had been serving in the military overseas. She'd been left with four kids and not a lot of money. Colton's office led a back-to-school backpack drive every year in part to make sure her children never went without. Gert always beamed with pride when delivering those items.

Gert organized a toy drive every year for Christmas, a book drive twice a year and coats for kids before the first cold snap.

"Hey, Trudy. You have a patient who just got out of surgery, and we'd like to go up to his floor and talk to his nurse and possibly his doctor," Colton said after introducing Trudy to Makena.

"Just a second, Sheriff. I'll look that up right now," Trudy said with a smile. Her fingers danced across the keyboard.

Makena's gaze locked onto someone. Colton followed her gaze to the man in scrubs. The doctor came from the same hallway they'd entered the lobby from, and then headed straight toward a bank of elevators.

The hair on Colton's neck prickled. Trudy's fingers worked double time. Click-click-click.

As the elevators closed on the opposite side of the lobby, something in the back of Colton's mind snapped.

"The patient you're looking for is on the

seventh floor. He's in critical condition. No visitors are allowed." She flashed eyes at Colton. "No normal visitors. That doesn't mean you. He's in room 717."

Colton thanked her for the courtesy and realized what had been sticking in the back of his mind. The doctor who'd crossed the lobby wore a surgical mask and regular boots. Every doctor Colton had seen had foot coverings on their shoes. They usually wore tennis shoes with coverings over them for sanitation purposes.

This guy had on a surgical mask and no boot covers?

One look at Makena said she realized something was up. Colton looked at Trudy before jumping into action the minute he made eye contact with Makena and realized she was thinking along the same lines.

"Trudy, call security. Send backup to the seventh floor and help to room 717."

Colton linked his fingers with Makena and started toward the elevator. Of course, he had a deputy on-site and the hospital had its own security. So imagine his shock when the elevator doors opened and his deputy walked out.

"Lawson, what are you doing?"

His deputy seemed dumbfounded as Colton rushed into the elevator.

"What do you mean? I'm going to get a cup of coffee. Hospital security relieved me and said you authorized a break."

"And you didn't think to check with me first?" Colton asked.

Lawson's mistake seemed to dawn on him. He muttered a few choice words as he pushed the button for the seventh floor, apologizing the whole time.

It seemed to take forever for the elevator to ding and the doors to open. At least, they knew where one of the men was; the other had to be close by. The two seemed to travel as a pair.

As soon as the doors opened, Colton shot out. He shouted back to Lawson, "Make sure no one comes down this hallway."

There were two hallways and several sets of stairs, but Lawson could make sure no one followed Colton.

Unwilling to let Makena out of his sight, Colton held on to her hand as he banked right toward room 717. As suspected, there was no security guard at the door.

Colton cursed as he bolted toward the open door.

Inside, he interrupted a man in a security outfit standing near River's bedside. The man in uniform had a black mustache, neatly trimmed.

"Sheriff, I saw him. Someone was in here. He ran out the door."

"Put your hands where I can see them," Colton demanded.

Chapter Sixteen

From behind the curtain dividing the room, a window leading to the outside opened.

"Hands where I can see them," Colton repeated, weapon drawn, leading the way. River lay unconscious with a breathing tube in his mouth as multiple machines beeped.

The security guard dropped down on the opposite side of the bed. And then, suddenly, an alarm began to sound on one of the machines. Was it unplugged?

Another wailing noise pierced the air.

Colton kept Makena tucked behind him as he took a couple of steps inside the room. He planted his side against the wall, inching forward.

A nurse came bolting in and froze when she saw Colton with his gun drawn. The divider curtain blew toward him with a gust of wind. Colton saw a glint of Mustache as he climbed out the window.

Red must've been on the other side of the divider all along. He must've made it inside the room. Colton assumed he'd be the one wearing the surgical gear.

"Freeze." Colton took a few more tentative steps before squatting down so he could see underneath the curtain. He saw no sign of shoes and assumed both men had climbed out the window and onto the fire escape they'd seen earlier. And since assumptions in his life of work could kill, he proceeded with extra caution. Someone could be standing on the bed or nightstand. Hell, he'd caught a perp climbing into the ceiling tiles at the bank before.

There was no more sound coming from that side of the room. He took a few more steps until he was able to reach the curtain and pull it open. He scanned the room before checking on the other side of the bed.

"Clear. Nurse, you're okay." It was all Colton could get out as he heard the sounds of feet shuffling and her scurrying to plug in the machines that were most likely the reason River was still breathing.

Colton rushed to the window and looked out in time to see someone wearing scrubs along with Security Dude climbing down the fire escape and around the side of the building.

He glanced back at Makena.

"Stay here. Someone will come back for you. Stay in this room. Nurse, lock this room and stay with her. As soon as I'm out of this window, I want you to lock it."

A moment of hesitation crossed Makena's features. She opened her mouth like she was about to protest and then clamped it shut.

Colton climbed out the window and followed the path of the perps. He climbed down to the corner, stopping before risking a glance.

The second he so much as peeked his head a shot rang out, taking a small chunk of white brick before whizzing past his face.

Colton quickly jerked back around the side of the building and pulled himself back up. His body was flat against the building, his weapon holstered.

There was no way these guys were escaping him twice.

He scaled the wall a couple more floors, refusing to look down. He wouldn't exactly say he was afraid of heights, but he wouldn't call them his friend, either.

When Colton made it to the third story,

gripping the windows for dear life, he risked another glance around the side of the building, hoping they would still be looking for him on the seventh floor. This time, thankfully, Red and Mustache were too busy climbing down to realize he'd looked. They probably still thought he was up on the seventh.

Colton continued his climb down with his stomach twisted in knots, but he made it to the ground. Without a doubt, they'd made it to the ground first. There were also two of them and only one of him. Not the best odds. One was a sharp-shooter. That would be the person who would most likely wield the weapon.

And then there was the fact that they were both cops. Maybe he could find a way to use that to his advantage.

With his back against the wall and his weapon extended, Colton leaned around the building. The pair of men were making a beeline for the parking lot. He scanned the area for the Jeep but didn't see it.

They could have another vehicle stashed by now. Since it was early evening, there was a little activity. He wouldn't risk a shot. He, like every law enforcement officer on the job, was responsible for every bullet he fired. Meaning that if he accidentally struck a citizen, he was answerable, not to mention it would be horrific.

When Red and Mustache made it to the lot, one turned around.

They took cover behind a massive black SUV. One turned back, Red, and Colton figured that of the two, he was the marksman. He had his weapon aimed at the seventh floor, where he must expect Colton to be.

He figured Mustache was looking for a vehicle to hotwire, since they didn't immediately go to a car.

Colton figured his best line of defense was to get to his county-issued vehicle and try to circle around the back and come at them from a different direction. He got on his radio to Lawson and Gert as he bolted toward his SUV.

He slid into the driver's seat and blazed around the opposite side of the lot as he informed Gert of the situation. Lawson chimed in, stating that he was on his way down and heading to the spot Colton had just left.

Colton slowed his SUV down to a crawl as he made his way around the back of the parking lot. He located a spot in the back of the lot and parked. He slipped out of his windbreaker, needing to shed anything that drew attention to him. He toed off his boots as he exited the vehicle.

As the shooter's attention was directed at the building, Colton swung wide to sneak up on him. He was ever aware that Mustache was creeping around the lot, likely looking for a vehicle.

Lawson peeked his head around the

building and Red fired a shot. While Red's attention was on Lawson, Colton eased through cars and trucks.

With Red distracted by Lawson, Colton came in stealth. He rounded the back of the SUV and dove at Red, tackling him at the knees. His gun went flying as Colton wrestled him around until his knee jabbed in the center of Red's back. As tall and strong as Red was, he was no match for a man of Colton's size.

Face down, Red spit out gravel as he opened his mouth to shout for help. Colton delivered a knockout punch. The man's jaw snapped.

From there, Colton was able to easily haul Red's hands behind his back and throw on zip cuffs.

It was then that Colton heard the click of a gun's hammer being cocked.

"Make one move without me telling you to, and you're dead."

Out of the corner of his eyes, Colton

could see Mustache. He cursed under his breath.

"Hands in the air where I can them." Mustache was in authoritative cop mode.

Colton slowly started lifting his hands, his weapon already holstered. And at this rate, he was as good as dead. His thoughts jumped to Lawson. Where was he?

"Uncuff my friend. You're going to help me get him into my vehicle."

The retort on Colton's lips was, *like hell.* However, he knew better than to agitate a cop on the edge.

"You won't get away with this. Your superiors know what you've done and they know you're connected to Myers. But you can get a lighter sentence. You haven't dug a hole that you can't climb out of yet. No one's dead. A murder rap is not something you can ever come back from."

"Shut up. I don't need to hear any more

of your crap. The system pays criminals better than it pays us. When Bic's kid needed medical care and his insurance ran out, who do you think covered his mortgage?" Stitch grunted. "It sure as hell wasn't the department."

Psychological profiles were performed on every officer candidate to ensure a cop could handle the pressures that came with the job. The tests could give a snapshot of where a candidate's head was at the time of his or her hiring. What it couldn't do 100 percent accurately was predict how someone would handle the constraints of the job over time.

The stress could compound and end up looking something like this.

"I never said it was easy being on the job. But you and I both know you didn't get into it for the money."

Mustache laughed. "Yeah, I was a kid. What did I know about having real bills and a father-in-law with dementia who lost his business and I had to support?"

"This isn't the answer. You can still make this right. You can still go back and untangle this. Make restitution."

A half laugh escaped Mustache.

"You know what? I think I'm just going to kill you instead. Not because I have to but because I can."

Colton had no doubt Mustache was trigger-happy. A man with nothing to lose was not the kind of person Colton needed to have pointing a gun at him.

"You're going to help me put my friend in my vehicle and then I'm going to give you ten seconds to run."

Colton knew without a doubt that the minute he put Red into a vehicle, his life was going to be over. He needed to think fast. Stall for time. He glanced over to see if Lawson was on his way.

Mustache laughed again.

"Your friend isn't coming. I don't know

if you noticed but he's bleeding out over there. Guess it's too late for me after all."

Colton slowly stood with his hands in the air.

"Keep high and where I can see them. I'm going to relieve you of your weapon."

The crack of a bullet split the air.

Colton flinched and dropped to his knees. When he spun around, it was Mustache taking a couple of steps back. With his finger on the trigger, all it would take was one twitch for Colton to be shot at in point-blank range.

He dove behind the sport utility and came up with his weapon. It would take Mustache's brain a few minutes to catch up with the fact that he'd been shot. Right now, he was just as dangerous as he had been, if not more so.

Using the massive sport utility for cover, Colton drew down on Mustache.

"Hands up, Stitch." All Colton could

think of was securing the area and getting to Lawson.

Another shot sounded.

Colton glanced around and saw Lawson's body. As he rounded the back of the vehicle, he heard a familiar voice.

"Drop your weapon *now.*" From behind a vehicle, Makena had her arms extended out with a Glock in her hands. Red's weapon? The barrel was aimed at Mustache.

Colton was proud of the fact she'd listened to his earlier advice and used the vehicle to protect her body.

Mustache seemed dumbfounded as he took a couple of steps and locked onto her position. "You."

He brought up his weapon to shoot her and she fired again. This time, the bullet pinged his arm and his shoulder drew back. His weapon discharged, firing a wild shot, and his shoulder flew back. His Glock went skittering across the black tar.

Colton dove toward it and came up with it after making eye contact with Makena. He tucked and rolled on his shoulder and then popped up in front of the vehicle Makena used as cover.

There was no way to know if Mustache had a backup weapon, which many officers carried in an ankle holster.

"You just saved my life," Colton said to Makena. He moved beside her and realized that her body was trembling.

Her eyes were wide.

"You're okay," he said to soothe her before turning to Mustache, who was slumped against the back tire of a vehicle. "Get those hands up."

Much to his surprise, Mustache did.

It was probably the shock of realizing he'd been shot multiple times. Colton immediately fished out his cell and called Gert, telling her the perps had been subdued and that Lawson was down. She reassured Colton a team of doctors was waiting at the ER bay for word.

Before Colton could end the call, he saw the doctors racing to save Lawson's life.

Mustache's once light blue shirt was now soaked in red. Colton ran over and cuffed Mustache's hands. After a pat-down, he located a backup weapon.

"If either one of these men moves, don't hesitate to shoot," he said to Makena.

Lawson was flat on his back as he was being placed on a gurney.

"I'm sorry. I let you down," Lawson said.

"No, you didn't. I'm alive. You're alive. Those bastards are going to spend the rest of their lives behind bars. You did good."

In less than a minute, Lawson was on his way to surgery. The bullet had nicked his neck.

Colton bolted back to Makena.

"It's over," Makena said. She repeated herself a couple more times as Colton took her weapon before he pulled her into an embrace, keeping a watchful eye on the perps.

"You did good," he whispered into her ear as she melted against him.

"I found the gun on the ground," she said quietly.

Red popped his head up and shook it, like he was shaking off a fog.

"What the hell happened?" His gaze locked onto his partner, who had lost a lot of blood.

"You and your partner are going away for a very long time," Colton said. He held Makena, trying to calm her tremors.

An emergency team raced toward Mustache. In another few minutes, he was strapped and cuffed to a gurney with security in tow and another deputy on the way.

Colton pulled Red to standing after patting him down. He walked the man over to his service vehicle. "You're taking a trip in the back seat for once."

Makena climbed into the passenger side and kept silent for the drive back to Katy Gulch.

Deputy Schooner met them in the parking lot and took custody of the perp.

"You would do what you had to if your kid was sick," Bic practically spat the words. "Look as sanctimonious as you want, but I had bills stacking up and a mortgage to cover. I did what was necessary to take care of my family."

"There are other ways to accomplish the same thing and stay within the law," Colton said.

"That's what you say. Don't you get tired of watching them get away with crimes every day? Don't you get sick of seeing criminals drive better cars and wear better clothes than us?"

"Fancy clothes were never my style," Colton said. "But why River?"

"He was on to us, so we turned the tables on him. His nose wasn't clean, either. He liked to play it rough," Bic said. "She was the problem. She threatened everything we were doing. It took months to track her down but she made mistakes and River led us right to her."

Colton was done talking. He turned to Makena. "Are you ready to go home?"

She stood there, looking a little bit lost.

"I don't have a home to go to, Colton."

"Then come home with me while you figure out your next move." He brushed the backs of his fingers against the soft skin of her face. He'd missed his opportunity with her once and did not intend to do so again. "Come home with me and stay."

"And then what?" She blinked up at him, confused.

"Stay. Meet my boys. See what you

think about making a life together. I know what I want and it's you. I love you, Makena. And I think I have since college. I was too young and too dumb to realize what was happening to us in college. I had no idea how rare or special it was. But I do now. I'm a grown man and I won't make that same mistake twice."

He looked into her eyes but was having trouble reading her. Maybe it was too much. Maybe he shouldn't have thrown this all at her at once.

"But if you don't think this is right, if you don't feel what I'm feeling, then just stay with me until you get your bearings. I don't care how long. You'll always have a place to stay with me."

"Did you say that you love me?"

Colton nodded. "Yes, Makena. I love you."

"I love you, too, Colton. I think I always have. Seeing you again brought me back to life. But then what? You have boys. You have a life."

"I'd like to build a life with *you*."

"Are you sure about that, Colton? Because I have no doubts."

"I've never been more certain of anything in my life other than adopting my boys," he admitted.

She blinked up at him, confused.

It dawned on him why. He'd never told her about his twins.

"Rebecca and I had been high school sweethearts. We didn't know anything but each other. We decided to take a break in college and see if this was the real deal. I loved her and she was my best friend. But then I met you and it was different. I felt things that I had never felt with Rebecca. There was a spark inside me that said you were special and then I wanted more than a best friend as a partner. I went home and told Rebecca that I didn't think I was coming back to her."

"But you ended up together?"

"Yes, but not for years. We went our separate ways as a couple but stayed close as friends. Years later, long after she and I broke up, she ended up in a bad relationship with a man who didn't treat her right. When he found out she was pregnant he accused her of cheating on him. He questioned whether or not the boys were his and that crushed her. She said she couldn't come home pregnant to her father's house without a husband or a father for her kids. We'd always promised to have each other's back, so that's what I did. Her father, who's the mayor of Katy Gulch, got over the fact she was pregnant and still not married as soon as he found out she was marrying an O'Connor. I felt like I could've done a lot worse than marry my best friend. I figured that what you and I had was a one-and-done situation. So I asked Rebecca to marry me. I loved her, but there was no spark in our marriage, not like what I'd experienced with you. But then, no one else made me feel that way. And make no mistake about it, those boys are my sons. They are O'Connors through and through, and always will be. Can you live with that?"

"Colton, you are the most selfless man I've ever met. I think I just fell in love with you even more."

"Just so you're clear, we can take a little time for you to get to know the boys, and we can make certain this is the life you want. But I'm in this for the long haul, and I have every intention of asking you to be my bride," he said.

"If your sons are half the person you are, I already know that I'll love them. And just so you know, when you ask me to marry you, I'll be ready to say yes. I never felt like I was home around anyone until I met you and then I lost it. I've definitely been in the wrong relationship and that taught me exactly what I wanted in a person. And it's you. It's always been you."

Colton pulled Makena into his arms and kissed his future bride, his place to call home.

"I have one condition," she warned.

"Anything." He didn't hesitate. He wanted to give her the world.

"You asked me before if I had any idea what I wanted to do once I had my freedom back."

He nodded.

"I want to volunteer at the motel to help out Peach. She told me about her and her husband building that place together and that the motel made her feel closer to him. She's considering selling, but I could tell nothing in her heart wanted that to happen. It would cut her off from the man she built a life with and she deserves so much more than that. She deserves to have her memories of him surrounding her until she takes her final breath."

"It sounds like the perfect plan to me." Colton kissed his future, his soon-to-be bride, his home.

Epilogue

"I have news."

Makena sat on the kitchen floor, playing with her favorite boys in the world. She'd taken them into her heart the minute she'd looked at those round, angelic faces. Someday, she wanted to expand their family, but after living with twins 24/7 for the past month, she realized her hands were full.

"What is it?" she asked Colton as he walked into the kitchen wearing only jeans hung low on his hips. He was fresh from the shower, hair still wet. Droplets rolled down his neck and onto his muscled chest.

She practically had to fan herself.

"Myers has agreed to testify against Bic, who will be put away a very long time for attempted murder and police corruption, among other charges."

Stitch hadn't made it, but Bic was the brains of the operation.

"Good for him," she said. "I'm so ready to close that chapter of my life. I'm done with running scared and I'm done hiding. He put me through hell and I'm just ready to move on and never look back."

Colton walked over to her and sat down behind her, wrapping his arms around her. He feathered kisses along the nape of her neck, causing her arms to break out in goose bumps and a thrill of awareness to skitter across her skin.

"I can't wait to be alone after we put the boys to bed tonight," he whispered in her ear.

She smiled as she turned her head enough for him to find her lips. The kiss sent more of that awareness swirling through her. Tonight felt like a lifetime away.

One of the boys giggled, which always made the other one follow suit. Their laughs broke into the moment happening between Makena and Colton.

"What's this?" she asked as she witnessed one pick up a block and bite it before setting it down only for the other to copy him.

Laughter filled the room and her heart.

This was her family. These were her boys. This was her home.

* * * * *